I NEED YOU FOR NEW YEAR'S

LYNN LARKIN

ALAUDAE PRESS

For my mom

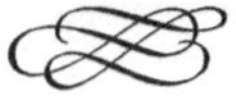

Erica Evans hovered outside Harrison's corner office, waiting for him to finish his call. Sweat beaded along the outside of the iced Americano in her left hand, leaving her palm wet and clammy. She sipped the peppermint mocha in her right hand, trying to rein in her nerves. She was, without a doubt, the best person for the job. Now, she just had to make her boss see it, too.

"Good luck, Erica. You've got this!" Pauline said as she walked by.

"Thanks," Erica gave Pauline a tight smile, wishing she hadn't announced her intentions to the entire events department earlier this morning. She'd been full of confidence then, but now it was dawning on her that Harrison might say 'no.' The idea of walking back on all that bravado made her cringe. Just one more reason failure was not an option.

"Erica, come on in," said Harrison. This was it. She took a deep breath and stepped into the CEO's office.

"What can I do for you?" he asked, waving his arm at a chair across from his desk.

"I wanted to talk to you about Madeline's job." She handed him the iced coffee.

"Thanks! I didn't have time to get one of these today." Harrison smiled and brought the straw to his lips.

Erica set her own drink on the edge of the desk before taking a seat.

"So, Madeline's job, huh?" Harrison leaned back in his chair. "I can't believe she's leaving. She's going to be tough to replace."

"Yeah, she is." Erica wiped her hands on her black pencil skirt, noting both were a little clammy now. She was young to take over the agency's events department, but she poured her heart and soul into this company. She was ready for this.

"So, I'm guessing you want some input into who the new Director of Events is going to be?" Harrison reached for his coffee again.

Erica swallowed down her disappointment. She knew she was going to have to convince him, but that didn't stop a part of her from hoping he'd see her as the logical candidate before she even asked.

"Actually, I was hoping you'd consider me for the job." Her fingers found the ends of her long blonde hair and started to twirl. So much for sounding confident.

Harrison sighed and shifted in his chair. "In two years, I'd promote you, no question. Even in one year, maybe. I'm just not sure you're ready yet."

Erica realized she was twirling her hair again—ugh, she hated that habit. Forcing her hand to her lap, she looked Harrison straight in the eye. "I know I don't have the years of experience, but I know this agency, and I'm great at what I do. I'm the right person for the job."

"Erica—" Harrison began. He was about to say 'no'. She knew it.

"Look, Harrison, if you hire someone else, the chances of the position being open when I'm ready in a year or two are slim to none. Are you willing to lose me to another agency, then?" She didn't plan to say it. She wasn't even sure she meant it.

Erica loved this place. She started here as a fresh-out-of-college intern and worked her way up the ranks. The agency was small enough that she knew everyone. Her colleagues—including Harrison—were like family. But the words were already out of her mouth, and all she could do was press forward. "I don't want to leave, Harrison. Just give me a chance."

Harrison leaned his elbows on the desk and placed his chin in his hand, his index finger rubbing over his mouth as he considered her request. She resisted the urge to twirl her hair again as she waited for him to reply.

"Alright. Here's the deal," he finally said. "I got a request today from the Calix Collection."

Erica sucked in a breath. The Calix Collection was Cade's family's hotel chain. A familiar spike of pain blossomed in her chest—the same one that hit her every time she thought of him. She shoved those memories down as best she could and tried to focus on what Harrison was saying.

"They want us to help them throw a New Year's Eve party that sells out and puts them on the map as a food and nightlife spot. I was about to turn them down, but I'd love to have them as a client. It could be a good opportunity for you to prove you have what it takes to lead the events team."

"I didn't realize Cade's family had a hotel in the area."

"Yeah, they converted the old Harbor Hotel into a Calix a

few months ago." Harrison gave her a strange look. "How do you know Cade Whitmore?"

"I don't, not really." Erica tried to brush it off, but Harrison narrowed his eyes at her, and she knew she wasn't getting off that easily.

"We had a thing in high school. No big deal." Erica pasted a smile on her face and shrugged, hoping it looked casual, even though it felt like a pound of lead rested on her shoulders.

"You sure? The look on your face says otherwise."

Normally, she loved that the owner of her agency knew her so well—it was probably the only reason he was giving her this chance at all. Right now, though, she hated it. She was here to convince him to give her a promotion, not to talk about her ex-boyfriend.

"Positive. I just haven't heard that name in a while. It'll be fine." Erica injected her voice with enough confidence that she believed her own words. It *would* be fine. It had to be. This promotion was too important.

Cade Whitmore had already destroyed her heart beyond repair. She wouldn't let him screw up her career, too. Besides, she was pretty sure he was still in London. Just because his family owned the hotel didn't mean he'd have anything to do with this event.

"Okay, so a New Year's Eve party." Erica steered the conversation back to the project. "As in, four weeks from now?" Her mind began to wrap itself around the details of an event like this. Under normal circumstances, she'd start planning at least three months ahead. She ran through the things that needed to happen in her head. It would be tight, but it wasn't impossible.

"I know, it's a crazy ask. With Madeline on her way out, I

didn't see how we'd make it work. But we're ahead on a few projects, so PR and Marketing should have time to pitch in. And if you're willing to put in the extra hours, I think we can do it." He took another drink of his coffee. "So, what do you say? Are you in?"

"Just to be clear, if I pull this off, I get the promotion?"

Harrison nodded.

Erica smiled as a thrill of victory washed over her. "Alright then. I'm in."

He was giving her a chance, and she wouldn't let him down.

CHAPTER 2

Cade Whitmore frowned at his phone as it buzzed with yet another incoming text from Katie, his date from last night. He leaned back in his desk chair, taking in the view of Tampa Bay as he debated how to respond. They'd only been out a few times, but he already knew he would be the one to break it off. Not that he didn't enjoy her company. Quite the opposite, actually. But getting tangled up in a relationship wasn't on his agenda.

It took him way too long to pick up the pieces last time.

He knew the rate at which he blew through women contributed to his playboy image. The reputation was unfounded—it wasn't like he was taking them all back to his room. But giving another woman access to his heart wasn't an option. Better to keep things casual and cut his losses as soon as either party started to catch feelings.

He plucked at an empty branch on the Christmas tree that his assistant, Jillian, set up in his penthouse suite a few mornings ago, still trying to decide how to phrase his response. She was supposed to bring ornaments too, but they hadn't materialized yet.

Cade's phone buzzed again, this time with an incoming call instead of a text. He was about to send Katie straight to voicemail, but seeing it was his dad calling, answered instead. "Hey, Dad, what's up?"

"Cade, how's the hotel coming? All set up for the grand opening of the rooftop bar?" As usual, his dad dove straight into business. Just once, Cade wished the conversation would start with a 'hey Cade, how are you?' instead, but he brushed that thought away quickly. He knew his dad loved him. Calvin Whitmore was just a to-the-point kind of guy, and no amount of wishing on Cade's part would change that.

"We're getting there. Construction is almost wrapped. We're just waiting for the light fixtures, which I'm told will arrive this week. Jillian lined up an events agency to plan the actual party." Cade stood up and paced around the suite as he filled his dad in.

"Was the New Year's Eve angle Jillian's idea?"

"Actually, it was mine." Cade rolled his eyes. He shouldn't have brought up Jillian. His dad never failed to hide his thoughts on Cade's 'overqualified, overpaid assistant.'

"It's smart," his dad said. "Even if it means you can't spend the holidays at home—"

"Dad." Cade cut him off. "I've already been over this with Mom. I'll be there for Christmas. I just can't stay long."

"Actually, that's what I wanted to talk to you about. Your mom and I decided that if you can't be here more than one full day, we'll just come to you. It won't hurt us to have a little warm weather for the holidays."

"Really?" Cade's face stretched into a grin. He was excited to see his parents. They'd always been a close family unit, and his mom had a knack for making the holidays special no matter what their location.

"Yeah, we'll fly in on the Friday before Christmas and stay through New Year's. That way, we'll get to see your grand opening." Cade heard the pride in his dad's voice and hoped his work lived up to it. The Calix hotels weren't just money-makers to his father—they were his life's work. His dad's presence meant more pressure to make everything perfect, but he had this handled.

"That sounds great, Dad. I'll let the front desk know so they can reserve a suite for you and mom. I'm really glad you're coming down."

"Us too, son."

The landline on his desk rang. Cade glanced at the clock and realized his next appointment was probably here. "I've gotta run to a meeting. I'll talk to you soon, though, Dad."

"Sure thing, Cade. Love you."

"Love you, too." When he first stared working for the hotel, Cade balked at any show of emotion while working. He didn't want to remind people he was getting special treat-ment because his dad owned the place. But after being on his own in London for two years, he appreciated the confirma-tion he was part of a family who loved him.

He ended the call with his dad and hit the speaker button on the landline.

"Hey Jillian," he said.

"The event planner is here to talk to you about New Year's. Do you want me to send her up, or get her settled in a conference room?" The background noise told him Jillian was on her cell phone in the hotel lobby.

"Conference room, please. It'll be easier to give her a tour of the event space if we start there." The event space was on the rooftop, and though Cade's suite was right below it, the elevator to the rooftop bar didn't stop anywhere but the lobby. Plus, Cade wanted to escape his room for a bit. His suite doubling as his office was convenient, but it also made him stir crazy.

"You've got it." Jillian hung up without saying goodbye. He loved how efficient she was. She'd been working with him for the last three years, following him from hotel to hotel. At this point, he wasn't sure what he'd do without her. His dad was right. She was overqualified to be his assistant, but as long as he paid her fairly for her talent, she seemed content to stay in the role. He planned on keeping her as long as he could.

Cade stood and grabbed the navy blue suit jacket off the back of his chair, pulling it on as he headed for the door. Sighing, he waited for the slowest elevator in the universe to make its way to the top of the building. They should add elevator upgrades to the renovations list. It was surprising how many guest surveys indicated streamlined elevator service could make or break a hotel stay.

The elevator finally arrived and carried him downstairs. He weaved his way through the lobby to the smallest of the three conference rooms.

The woman inside typed intently on her laptop, not looking up, even though he was sure she heard him enter. Her side was to him, and a strand of hair that escaped her bun covered part of her face, but he'd know that profile anywhere. Erica Evans, the only girl he'd ever loved.

A whoosh of air left his lungs. What was she doing here?

He should go sit down, but his legs were frozen where he stood in the doorway.

"Erica, I'd like to introduce you to Cade Whitmore, our

hotel manager and the brains behind this New Year's party." Jillian said from her seat across from Erica. "Cade, this is Erica, our event planner for New Year's."

He managed to school his features into a neutral expression before Erica turned, her mouth forming a surprised 'O' as she took him in. She looked the same, except not. She'd gone from girl to woman since he last saw her, but she was more beautiful than ever. And judging by the look on her face, she was as surprised to see him as he was to see her.

CHAPTER 3

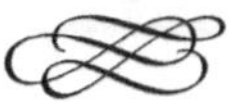

Erica's lungs stopped taking in air as she stared at the man before her. He looked good, but that was no surprise. She'd seen his photographs online—him with a different girl each night as he explored the nightlife in New York, then London. She realized her mouth was still hanging open and snapped it shut.

So what if he was still the most attractive man she knew? He left her. He'd moved on, and so had she. But then, why did it feel like her heart was breaking all over again? What was Cade even doing here? He was supposed to be in London.

"We've...met." Cade said, pulling her out of her mental spiral. His voice was deeper now, but it still sounded like him.

His assistant looked between them curiously. Erica didn't envy her. She had no idea what she'd stepped into by hiring Erica's agency to organize and promote this event.

Erica's gaze flicked back to Cade. His facial expression was impassive, a look he must have mastered since the last time she saw him, because she'd been able to read his every emotion when they were together.

Or maybe he was just that unaffected by seeing her.

The thought bothered her more than she liked to admit. She should be glad he wasn't freaking out. At least this way, he wouldn't fire her on the spot. She hoped.

This event was her one and only chance at the promotion. If Cade didn't want to work with her, she was screwed.

Her skin tingled as she fought the urge to flee the room. It didn't matter that being this close to him made it so she couldn't breathe. This was her assignment, and she had to complete it.

"Can I get either of you coffee or water?" Jillian stood and headed toward the door.

A fresh wave of panic washed over Erica at the thought of being left alone with Cade. Would he bring up their past, or would he ignore it? She wasn't sure which was worse.

"Nothing for me, but could you point me to the nearest restroom?" Erica stood, smoothing her skirt.

Inhale. Exhale. Flipping her laptop shut, she forced herself to breathe as she followed Jillian to the door.

"The ladies' room is down that hall. It'll be the second turn on the right."

Erica thanked her and fled, walking as fast as her three-inch pumps and tight pencil skirt allowed. She wasn't sure whether to laugh, scream or cry, but she'd vowed a long time ago not to give Cade Whitmore any more of her tears.

With that in mind, she pulled her anger around her like a protective shield. Who had she pissed off so badly in a past life that the trajectory of her career depended on her ability to work through the holidays with her ex?

Holding onto to the bathroom sink, she forced herself to take a deep breath.

In through the nose.

Out through the mouth.

She stared at her reflection in the mirror, willing her features into their usual client-facing mask. She was a fantastic event planner. Unforeseen curve balls didn't phase her; she dealt with them every day. Her ability to stay cool in the middle of a crisis had impressed more than one client, and it was probably the only reason Harrison was considering her for this promotion.

This wasn't even a real curve ball.

She just had to stay professional and treat Cade like any other client. Erica steeled herself in the mirror, then left the restroom with her back straight and her head held high.

"WHAT WAS THAT ALL ABOUT?" Jillian asked, once Erica disappeared down the hall.

Cade shrugged. He wasn't sure himself. It had been ten years, but he could still read her like a book. Surprise, hurt, panic, determination, and sadness all made an appearance before she raced out of the room like she was on fire.

"You two obviously know each other," Jillian said.

Cade rubbed a hand over his face. "We dated in high school."

Jillian raised an eyebrow, waiting for him to elaborate further. He didn't. As much as he liked his assistant, he wasn't about to dive into his feelings on Erica Evans with her. Especially now, when Erica could arrive back from the bathroom at any moment. It was obvious Erica left to go collect herself, but why she needed to was beyond him. She'd been the one to end things all those years ago.

He picked up his phone and tapped the corner gently against the table. It was on the tip of his tongue to ask Jillian to choose a different agency—or at least a different event planner—but Erica was back before he could get the words out.

He felt her presence like a storm in the air. One glance at her face confirmed the kaleidoscope of emotions was gone. Now, she looked coolly detached, her normal expressions masked by a pasted-on smile.

"Sorry about that." Erica cleared her throat. "It seems like we have a lot to cover. Shall we dive right in?" She slid into the chair across from him and reopened her laptop.

When neither he nor Jillian objected, she continued. "Tell me about your vision for the New Year's party."

If she could act professional, so could he. Leaning forward in his seat, he rested his elbows on the table in front of him. "It's really the grand opening of our rooftop bar. But no one shows up for the grand opening of a hotel bar these days, so we thought making it a New Year's party would draw people in."

"Smart. Really smart," Erica said as she typed notes into her laptop. She looked up, but was careful not to look him in the eye. "Okay, so tell me about the space. What's the vibe you're going for with the rooftop bar in general? I'm thinking we'll want to lean into that for our theme, unless you had something else in mind?"

"No, that's exactly what I was thinking." Cade was thankful she got it right away. He'd been skeptical when Jillian hired an events agency, but he knew they needed help if they were going to pull this off in under a month.

Still, most event planners he'd dealt with in the past wanted to go way overboard in the theme department. If this turned into a hokey New Year's Eve party, they'd bring in the wrong crowd. He wanted to attract people who'd return for brunch or sunset cocktails, not a bunch of college kids looking for a dance party.

Then again, this was Erica. She'd been pulling off understated, but amazing events since she chaired their high school dance committee.

She nodded and typed more notes into her laptop.

"The whole rooftop has kind of a tropical garden vibe," He said, describing the bar in more detail. "Twinkle lights, comfy patio furniture, lots of plants, a DJ booth, and a dance area that holds a couple giant Jenga games during the day."

"That's great." Erica said, still not meeting his gaze. "Okay, so is the whole space outdoors?"

"It has an indoor component as well. We can open the whole thing up or close the glass sliders if the weather's bad."

Erica's fingers paused on their laptop keys as she cocked her head, thinking. He recognized that look. Her mind was whirling with ideas to make his bar opening epic. Despite their rocky history, the event was in good hands.

She continued to ask him questions about the space and the party as though he was any other client, never breaking that calm, professional tone.

Her cool demeanor bothered him, even though it shouldn't. He saw right through the fake smiles that didn't reach her eyes—eyes that used to light up whenever he walked into the room.

At least until she stopped taking his calls.

Yeah, no. This wasn't happening. He wasn't getting

sucked back into Erica-land. In fact, he'd let Jillian handle the party details from now on.

"How many tickets are you looking to—"

"I have another meeting to get to," Cade interrupted, pushing his chair back from the table. A look of surprise crossed Erica's face as he stood up, and he mentally congratulated himself on cracking that professional facade she'd been hiding behind.

Wait, why did he even care?

Being around her was messing with his head. He turned to his assistant. "Jillian, can you hammer out the rest of these details and show Erica the rooftop?"

"Uh, sure?" Jillian looked at him like he might be losing his mind, but thankfully didn't push him on it.

"Great, if there are any questions you can't answer, we can talk about them later." He paused at the door, then turned and added, "Good seeing you again, Erica."

He hurried toward the elevator, not sure whether he meant those parting words or not.

His phone buzzed with another text from Katie, this one letting him know she'd made other plans since she didn't hear from him. Well, that was disappointing. Somehow, his potential to develop feelings for her seemed a lot less dangerous now than it had this morning.

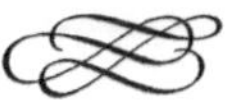

"I'm doing a food tasting at the Calix tomorrow. It's free lunch, if you want to come." Erica glanced at the menu on the wall of the salad shop, hoping the request sounded casual.

She'd been making excuses to take Pauline to the hotel with her for the last two weeks, not wanting to chance running into Cade alone. He hadn't made an appearance since that first meeting, but that almost made it worse. She could only brace herself for dealing with him if she knew it was coming. It was hard to say whether passing responsibility for the New Year's party to his assistant was standard practice, or a deliberate move to avoid working with her. Not that it mattered. She liked Jillian and would happily avoid spending any extra time with Cade.

"You know I hate to turn down free lunch, but I thought you wanted me in the office to keep an eye on the social media team." Pauline gave Erica a little nudge to keep up with the line. "We need to get those sponsored posts going ASAP if we want any chance of selling out."

"Ugh, you're right." Erica needed her in the office. They planned to sell just enough tickets to make it feel popular without overwhelming the bartenders. The only problem was, if they didn't sell out, it would feel empty.

Erica thought about sending Pauline to do the tasting while she oversaw the social media. But she'd already told Jillian she would be there, and she wanted to taste the food herself. Besides, Cade hadn't shown up to any of their other meetings. There was no reason to believe he'd come to this one.

She and Pauline placed their salad orders and carried their food to an empty table.

"Not that I mind," Pauline said as they sat down, "but you've been bringing me onsite with you way more than usual, and I'm not sure I'm adding anything. Given the short timeline, aren't we better dividing and conquering?"

Erica sighed. For someone who'd only been working a year and a half, Pauline was really sharp. "Would you believe me if I said I was trying to train you to do my job when I get promoted?"

"I'd like to, but I'm pretty sure I'm not qualified to run an entire event on my own yet. And, no offense, but you're not one to share your client visits. You practically had a showdown with Madeline last summer, when she asked you to let an intern shadow you." Pauline took a bite of her salad.

"That's because interns are wildcards." Erica took a bite of hers, savoring the taste of apple and goat cheese.

"Well, I'll take that as a compliment, I guess. But you have been acting a little weird about this event, and I'm not the only one who's noticed."

"Harrison?" Erica asked, setting her fork down.

"I overheard him and Madeline talking about it this morning. He said he hoped you weren't cracking under the pressure."

"This is so unfair!" Erica covered her face with her hands.

"What is?" Pauline looked at her with genuine concern—probably for her sanity.

Erica sighed. "Can you keep a secret?"

Pauline nodded and leaned forward, eyes sparkling with excitement at being in the know for once.

Erica glanced around, making sure no one else from their office was in the restaurant before saying, "Cade Whitmore and I dated in high school."

"Cade Whitmore, the Calix client?" Pauline's expression was a mixture of shock and awe.

"Yeah." Erica picked at a napkin.

"But wait," said Pauline. "Why is that even an issue? You guys dated, what, ten years ago? I bet if you told Harrison, he wouldn't even care."

"I did tell Harrison." The problem was, seeing Cade again made it feel like yesterday. "The issue isn't that we dated in high school. It was just a huge shock to see him sitting there in that conference room at the initial meeting. I thought he was still in London."

"Why do I sense there's more to the story? What happened between you two?"

Erica leaned forward. "If I tell you, you can't repeat it."

"I swear."

"Short version? Cade's family moved here my junior year. We started dating. I thought we were in love. We were all set to go to USF together and less than three weeks before we were set to move into our dorms, he told he was going to

Columbia instead. Like it was no big deal." She still remembered that conversation like it was yesterday. Standing on the beach, her heart cracking in half, waiting for Cade to tell her it was some kind of joke. But one look at his face told her everything she needed to know—he was leaving, and there was nothing she could do to change his mind.

She blinked back the tears that threatened to fall at the memory. She wasn't going to cry in front of Pauline. In fact, she wasn't going to cry at all. She'd given Cade enough of her tears. He wasn't getting any more.

"Anyway," she shook head as though it would clear away the memories of Cade. "Long story short, my promotion is now dependent on impressing my ex."

"Oof, that's rough." Pauline said, tilting her head like she was mulling something over. "You still have feelings for him, don't you?"

"No, I don't," Erica said, stabbing at a spinach leaf with her fork. "But he has a history of throwing wrenches into my plans, and I can't afford for this event to be anything but perfect."

If New Year's Eve went badly, she would lose out on the promotion—and everyone in the office would know she couldn't hack it.

A small smile crept over Pauline's face, making Erica frown harder.

"What? What are you smiling about?"

"It's just that it's kind of like one of those Hallmark holiday movies." Pauline took a drink of her iced tea.

She had to be joking.

"You know," Pauline went on, "girl has to work with ex-boyfriend to achieve her holiday goal and they live happily ever after."

"Give me a break. My life is *not* a holiday movie, and Cade and I lost our chance at a happily ever after a long time ago." Erica tossed down her fork, no longer hungry despite only finishing half of her lunch.

CHAPTER 5

Cade stood in the Calix lobby, coffee in hand, watching guests come and go. In some ways, the lobby of a Calix hotel was more like home for him than anywhere else. He grew up following his dad from one hotel to another, which meant more time in hotel lobbies than living rooms.

This was the first space they updated when he took over, and Cade found himself here often. As a kid, he'd make up imaginary stories about the people walking in and out. He still did it sometimes: The young couple holding hands were definitely newlyweds. The old man with a book in his hand and a sad look on his face was a lonely widower. The blonde woman in a navy dress was the gorgeous event planner he couldn't get out of his head—that one wasn't made up, though he wished it was.

Erica's gaze found his. He gave her a nod, then turned and headed for the elevator, glad he didn't have to meet with her today. Cade mentally congratulated himself for putting Jillian in charge of the event. His only regret was not doing it sooner.

If his parents weren't coming, he leave early for New York, spend the holidays there, and go straight to Utah for his annual college buddies' ski trip. By the time he got back to Tampa, the party would be over, and he could stop worrying about running into Erica.

Back in his penthouse suite, he placed an order for a power bowl from room service. The downfall of living in a hotel was not having a kitchen. The suite had a refrigerator and microwave, but no oven or stove. Room service might seem like a convenient option for a twenty-eight-year-old bachelor, but it always took a bunch of time, and the food was rarely hot when it arrived.

Still thinking of the ski trip, he dashed off a text to his college roommate.

Cade:

Hey, haven't seen you in the ski trip group chat lately. You're still coming, right?

There were five of them that went on the annual ski trip, and everyone but Nate had jumped into the group chat to say how excited they were.

Nate:

Sorry, man. I've been meaning to call you. I can't make it this year. Ashley and I are getting married in February and I can't take off work for both the ski trip and the honeymoon.

Cade sighed, disappointed he wouldn't see Nate. The other guys were fun, but catching up with his best friend between slopes was what kept him going back every year.

Nate:

You gonna be back in New York for Christmas?

Cade:

No. Parents are coming down to see me in Tampa instead.

Nate:

Shoot. I was hoping you'd have time for dinner or something with me and Ash.

With Cade being in London, then Tampa, he hadn't spent much time with Nate's fiancé. Once again, he regretted not passing the party off to Jillian sooner.

Cade:

You could always come here for New Year's. The hotel's doing a big event on the rooftop.

Cade didn't really expect Nate to come, but it'd be fun if he could.

Nate:

Actually, that sounds awesome. Ash was just complaining about how her sparkly dress and heels don't mix with the snow that's predicted here. Let me check with her.

Cade:

Seriously?

He smiled. With Jillian doing most of the heavy lifting for New Year's, he would be free to hang out with Nate and Ashley—if they came.

Nate:

thumbs-up emoji

Cade:

Awesome. Let me know when you talk to her.

Nate:

Will do.

A knock drew Cade's attention to the door. It was pretty fast for room service, but maybe he was lucky. Instead of his food, he found Jillian on the other side.

"Jillian, I thought you were—" Cade took in his assistant's puffy face and bloodshot eyes and knew he was about to encounter the opposite of luck. "What's wrong?"

"It's my mom." Jillian sniffed. "There was a car accident. She's in the hospital. Cade, it's not good. They put her in a medically induced coma. I need to go to New Jersey to be with her."

"Of course, Jill. Whatever you need," Cade said, meaning it. She was an employee, but she was also a friend.

"Thanks Cade." Jillian gave him a quick hug. "I'm going to see if I can catch the next plane out of here." She turned to leave, then spun back. "Oh, I totally forgot. Erica is here to decide on the menu. She and the chef are already waiting upstairs. Can you go cover for me?"

Cade's mind raced, trying to come up with a solution that didn't involve him spending time with Erica.

"Cade, you'll cover for me, right?" Jillian looked panicked.

"Yeah, yeah, of course. Go be with your mom." Cade tried to force a smile, but it came out feeling more like a grimace.

"Thanks, Cade." Jillian hit the elevator button, then pulled out her phone and dialed, probably calling the airline.

Cade's phone buzzed with an incoming text. The elevator arrived, but he made no move to get on with Jillian. Instead, he reached into his pocket to check his phone. He was in no rush to go to the tasting. If he was lucky, Erica would start without him, and he'd only have to make it through a few courses with her.

Nate:
Hey, just talked to Ash. We'll come in on the 27th and stay through New Year's. Think you'll be able to stop working long enough to show us around? Looking forward to it, man.

Well, at least Nate was coming in. Not that Cade would have much free time to hang out, with Jillian gone.

He pressed the down button on the elevator, wishing he could just call the whole New Year's party off. It was too late for that, though. Some of the tickets were already sold. And even if they weren't, having to explain to his dad why the rooftop bar wasn't opening as planned was even less appealing than spending an afternoon with his ex.

CHAPTER 6

Erica glanced at her watch and sighed. Jillian was almost twenty minutes late. She wasn't responding to calls or texts, either. Where was she?

For a second, Erica wondered if she had the date wrong. But the chef was here, too, looking just as confused as she was.

"Jillian did say noon today, right?" she asked.

"Yeah." He leaned against the wall next to a door that led to the kitchen. "You haven't heard from her yet?"

Erica shook her head. "No, she hasn't replied.

"The appetizers are sitting under a heat lamp. I would've liked to serve them fresh," he griped.

"The heat lamp is a good test of whether they'd hold up on a buffet." Erica tried to put a positive spin on things, even though she couldn't blame him for being annoyed.

He frowned. "They'd be better passed."

"Agreed. I'll see what I can do." She was hoping to have passed hors d'oeuvres to start, and a buffet later in the evening, but she hadn't confirmed that plan with Jillian. The big question was whether the hotel had enough servers available to do the passing.

Suddenly realizing she hadn't introduced herself yet, she stood up and offered him her hand. Just that glimpse of Cade in the lobby had tossed her off her game. She was thankful Jillian turned out to be her main point of contact for the event. She wasn't sure what she would do if she had to interact with Cade on a daily basis for the next two and a half weeks.

"I'm Erica, by the way."

"Will," he said, taking her hand and giving it a light shake. He was cute, she realized, taking in his blue eyes and dimples. His physique told her he spent considerable time in the gym.

That she failed to notice his attractiveness earlier was just more proof that being around Cade messed with her head. Erica would never date a hotel employee while she was planning an event, but that didn't usually stop her from noticing a hot guy when she saw one.

"Well, Will, it appears we've been stood up." Her stomach rumbled loudly, causing her to blush. She wouldn't have skipped breakfast this morning if she knew Jillian was going to be this late.

"You want to do the tasting without her?" Will asked, looking amused.

Erica hesitated, unsure what the protocol was here. She'd never had a client no-show to a tasting before.

"Sure," she said, finally. She was starving, and they didn't have the time to reschedule. Jillian would just have to be happy with whatever she picked.

"Come on back." Will held the door to the kitchen for her.

She grabbed her bag and followed him into the kitchen.

The commercial kitchen was full of gleaming stainless steel. Her eyes and nose drew her toward the heat lap, where several bite-sized snacks waited to be served. She reached for a chicken skewer.

"Hold up," Will said, pulling a tray out of the walk-in refrigerator. "Those have been sitting too long. I'm going to remake them."

Erica grudgingly put down the chicken skewer.

Will held up his hands, laughing. "You look like a wolf who just had her kill stolen."

Erica gave him a sheepish grin. "Sorry, I'm just starving."

"Go ahead and eat it if you want," he said, scooping bruschetta onto a crostini and sliding it toward her. "I'm just saying it'll taste better fresh."

"I'll trust you," Erica said, taking the plate of bruschetta from him and digging in. The flavor of fresh tomatoes and tangy garlic danced over her tongue.

"These are amazing," she said through a mouthful of food.

"Thanks," he laughed.

She made sure to finish chewing the bruschetta completely before speaking again. "So what's next?"

CHAPTER 7

Cade stepped off the elevator and looked around the empty dining room. Where was Erica? Had they finished already? He couldn't decide whether to be annoyed or relieved. It wasn't like he was looking forward to spending time with his ex, but standing alone in the empty restaurant, he couldn't help feeling like he'd been stood up.

He turned to leave, but changed directions when he heard laughter coming from the kitchen. When he got to the swinging door, he paused.

Through the window, he spotted Erica sitting on a folding stool, smiling at something the chef said. Cade loved that smile almost as much as he hated the stab of jealousy that it was directed at someone else. Chef Will stood across from her, mixing something in a bowl.

"I still think I should try the ones that have been sitting for a bit—just in case." Erica reached for one of the plates under the heat lamp.

Will said something about a she-wolf and Erica burst out

laughing. They'd known each other for less than an hour. How did they have an inside joke already?

Cade told himself he was just mad that he didn't get it. It didn't bother him at all that Erica was smiling and laughing with another guy. That would be ridiculous, considering they weren't together, and hadn't been for almost ten years.

Cade watched through the window as Erica tucked a strand of hair behind her ear. "No, really. Since Jillian isn't here to clarify, we should prepare for both options. This event has to be perfect, including the food."

He should head in there instead of eavesdropping, but he liked seeing her light and laughing like this. He had a feeling her good mood would evaporate the instant he walked in. It was pretty obvious she still had a chip on her shoulder where he was concerned.

"Not that I'm complaining about your desire to showcase my food at its best, but most people in your shoes would be like 'the client didn't show, so I'll eat my free lunch, pick a couple things, and it'll be good enough.' Why the pursuit of perfection?" Will set his bowl down and wiped his hands on his white apron. Clearly, the guy didn't know Erica. Even in high school, she never did anything halfway.

"I have a promotion riding on this event. I need it to be a success, so I'm leaving as little as possible to chance. Plus, this is the grand opening of your restaurant. If you want people to come back, the food has to be good."

Cade pushed open the swinging door to the kitchen, feeling guilty for lurking so long. He cleared his throat and steeled himself for Erica's icy response.

"Mr. Whitmore." Will nodded in his direction, still mixing whatever was in that bowl. "I didn't realize you'd be joining us."

"Please, call me Cade." He watched the happiness melt off Erica's face as she spun around to look at him. Even though he'd been expecting it, the loss of her smile made something tighten in his chest.

"I thought I was meeting Jillian." Erica's hand went to her necklace, and she began twisting the silver pendant between her fingers. She was always twirling either a necklace or her hair when she got nervous.

Cade found himself transported back to high school for a second, watching her twist the bow-shaped pendent on the necklace he gave her for Christmas senior year.

"Jillian had a family emergency. Looks like you're stuck with me instead." Despite the fact that it was his hotel, he felt out of place.

"Oh." Erica pressed her lips together, then pasted on that fake smile from their first meeting. "Well, have a seat, then."

Cade looked down pointedly at the lack of stool next to her.

"Let me go grab another stool." Will went to find one, leaving them alone for a minute.

"Erica, I—" Cade didn't know what he was planning to say, but he couldn't just ignore the elephant in the room. After all, they'd be working closely together now.

"Look, Cade, I know this is awkward, but let's not make it worse by digging up the past. Let's just keep things professional, okay? You're a client and I'm an event planner." Erica brushed some non-existent lint off her dress as she spoke.

"Fine by me." Cade took in the stiffness in her posture, the phony look on her face, and the way she still refused to meet his eyes. "But can you just be normal, then? This ice queen thing you've got going on is creeping me out." The words were out before he could stop them.

"I'm *creeping* you out?" The indignation in Erica's voice told Cade that he'd struck a nerve. Maybe that hadn't been the best thing to say, but at least it made her show some emotion.

"Kind of." Cade shrugged, unwilling to take it back.

Will returned empty-handed.

"Couldn't find an extra stool. Why don't you guys move out to the bar and I'll bring the rest of the food out there?"

"Sure," Cade said, feeling like he'd just broken up a party. He should have stayed in his suite with his power bowl.

Erica gathered her things and followed him out of the kitchen.

"Will and I think passed appetizers is the way to go," she said when they were seated at the bar in the dining room. "And then a buffet starting around nine o'clock." Her voice was even colder than before. He shouldn't have made the ice queen comment. "Is that possible with current waitstaff?"

"That should be fine," Cade said, knowing the restaurant manager was waiting on his okay before finalizing the New Year's Eve schedule. "Do you have any idea about the number of guests we can expect?"

"Jillian and I landed on selling one hundred twenty-five tickets, total," said Erica.

"Only one twenty-five? What about no-shows? Empty is almost worse than over-crowded." The restaurant seated a hundred guests, but it could hold a lot more when they weren't doing a sit-down meal.

"I know we can technically hold one sixty-five, but the bars aren't set up to serve that many at once, unless you're only serving a limited beer and wine selection. There's also a pool of friends and family tickets on top of the ones we're selling."

Cade nodded. Erica's reasoning was spot on, but her delivery was still ice cold.

Will emerged from the kitchen with two cocktail-sauce filled martini glasses, each with four shrimp along the edge. "Alright, first up, we've got the cold option—shrimp cocktail."

"This looks great!" Erica reached for a shrimp and dunked it into the sauce.

"Is this for passing, or later?" Cade asked, his eyes on Erica as she tilted her head back slightly and bit into the shrimp. He swallowed hard as he realized what a mistake it was to focus on her mouth. Her lips used to taste like frosting-flavored lip gloss. He wondered what they'd taste like now.

"Later." Will stepped back to allow them to taste his creation. "Erica already selected the appetizers, but I can make a few more for you, if you'd like?"

"No, that's alright. I'll trust my event planner." He turned his attention to his own shrimp. The cocktail sauce had an extra zing to it, and he nodded his appreciation to the chef, who headed back into the kitchen.

"Alright, so how close are we to sold out?" He asked Erica, trying to get his mind off her lips and back on the event.

"We've sold around forty tickets so far." Her voice stayed even and upbeat, though the number made Cade frown.

"That's… not great." New Year's Eve was just over two weeks away, and most people had their plans nailed down by Christmas. They could count on a few at-the-door sales from hotel guests, but that wouldn't be more than a handful of tickets.

"I've got my team working on social media today, and there's a local radio spot running a couple times this week.

We'll fill up." Erica said it with confidence, though Cade couldn't tell if it was real or the false bravado she seemed to have perfected sometime in the last ten years.

Will reappeared from the kitchen and set a platter down in front of them. "Next up, I thought we might showcase the sandwiches from the menu by serving mini-versions. We've got French Dip, Turkey Rueben, Pesto Portobello and Chicken Caesar Wrap. I thought about doing mini-sliders instead, but this showcases the restaurant menu better. I also made fries with our signature aioli."

"That sounds perfect," Erica said, reaching for a piece of French Dip. The sandwich was held together by a toothpick, and came with a tiny bowl of broth for dipping.

"Erica, you know that's beef, right?" The words were out of Cade's mouth before he could stop them. Erica didn't eat beef—at least, she hadn't in high school. His face flushed with embarrassment. It wasn't like his tastes hadn't changed in the last ten years. He looked away, wishing he could un-ask the question.

Will paused on his way back to the kitchen, probably waiting to hear whether he'd missed a food preference.

"Oh, yeah. I discovered in college that beef wasn't all bad," Erica said in her professional tone.

Cade shifted uncomfortably in his seat, realizing he didn't really know her anymore. Suddenly, he couldn't wait for this tasting to be done.

The corner of her mouth quirked up. "I still prefer fish to steak, and I can't stand the texture of beef burgers." She was smiling by the time she finished speaking. A real smile, not the pasted-on one he'd grown to hate. There was the Erica he knew.

Cade hid his own grin by taking a bite of one of the sandwiches.

"Are you still refusing to eat mayonnaise unless it's mixed with something else and called aioli?" Erica asked as he tentatively dipped a fry in the sauce.

"Yup," Cade said, popping the fry into his mouth. The sauce was good, despite Erica's reminder that it contained one of his least favorite ingredients.

For just a second, being there with her felt like old times.

"Did you guys want to try the desserts, too?" Will returned with a tray of eclairs and mini-cupcakes. At Erica's nod, he set the desserts on the bar and cleared the empty sandwich plates. "I'll just leave you to try these and discuss any changes you'd like made to the menu. Come grab me when you need me."

After choosing a cupcake, Erica turned in her seat to get a better view of the water.

"You know what would be really cool? A fireworks show over the water at midnight. I don't think it's possible to set that up in two weeks, but people would love it." Erica bit into the vanilla cupcake, leaving a smear of white frosting on her upper lip.

As though his hand had a mind of its own, Cade reached over and gently took her chin in his hand, swiping the frosting from her lip with his thumb. Touching her lip sent a series of tingles up his arm and down his spine.

Her eyes widened in shock, but they also reflected the desire he felt.

Without taking his eyes off hers, Cade slowly retracted his hand and licked the frosting from his thumb.

"What the heck was that?" Erica broke out of the trance a second before he did.

He wished he knew. He also wished he could take it back.

"Sorry, force of habit, I guess," he mumbled.

"Cade, I don't think I can do this." Erica's face crumpled. He could tell only her iron willpower was keeping her from tears.

"I'm sorry, Er. That was a mistake." Cade's chest tightened. Even now, he hated to see her upset.

"Thinking I could work with you was the mistake." Erica said, squeezing her eyes closed.

She took a deep breath, then stood up and grabbed her bag. "I need to go. Will you tell the chef you're good with the menu?"

"You're still going to finish this event, right?" Cade asked, panicking a bit.

Erica kept going toward the elevator and pressed the button.

"Right?" He projected his voice across the empty dining room.

He had a lot riding on this event, too, and there was no way he could do it by himself. He stood and took a few steps toward her.

She turned, tears glistening in her eyes. "I don't know," she said, and stepped onto the elevator.

"Well, I need you for New Year's, and based on what I overheard earlier, it sounds like you need this gig!" Cade half-shouted just before the elevator doors slid shut.

CHAPTER 8

Erica blinked back tears as the elevator descended, willing them to hold off until she made it through the lobby. They might not be streaming down her face yet, but the slight blur to her vision told her she didn't have long. She stepped out of the elevator and hurried through the lobby, bumping one woman with her shoulder and another with the large bag tucked under her arm.

"Sorry," she mumbled, without slowing down.

A single tear slid down her face as she pushed through the double doors that led to the pool deck. Skirting the pool, she headed toward the beach beyond. It wasn't long before she reached the sand. She kicked off her high-heeled pumps and stowed them in her tote. The salty air soothed her, just a little.

The beach was nearly empty—typical for December. Only the bravest tourists tried to swim in the bay this time of year. Those that wanted to swim at Christmas stuck to heated hotel pools and hot tubs. The few other people on the beach today weren't wearing swim attire, so she didn't look too out-of-place walking near the water in her dress.

She passed stacks of chairs and a pile of umbrellas that the hotel provided for guests. Despite the weather being pleasant, the stand that passed them out was closed. There probably weren't many guests at the hotel this week. They'd begin arriving next week, once schools let out for the holidays.

She walked without a conscious destination, but when she finally looked up, she suspected her feet knew where they were taking her all along. It was *their* spot. The place Cade broke her heart all those years ago.

Erica sat down under the palm tree—it was taller now than she remembered. She leaned back on her elbows and dug her hands into the sand, squeezing, then letting it drift through her fingertips. Eventually, the flow of tears slowed. She picked up her bag and dug through it until she found a packet of tissues. Plucking a few from the wrapper, she dabbed her face and blew her nose.

Cade's parting words echoed through her head. *From what I overheard, it sounds like you need this gig.*

The whole thing was so unfair. She *did* need this event, but why did her promotion have to be tied to Cade? She thought she could stay professional, but today's meeting had been anything but. In fact, Erica couldn't remember a time in her entire career that she'd made such a fool of herself in front of a client.

Granted, Cade started it.

She could still feel the tingle of his touch on her lip. What was he thinking, touching her like that?

And how had she just let him? She'd been paralyzed, stuck in an echo of a past that no longer existed. With a sigh, she sat up. She could deny it all she wanted, but this after-noon had shown her one thing for sure. She wasn't over Cade Whitmore.

She still hadn't decided what to do about that when she heard someone coming toward her across the sand.

"I didn't expect to find you here," Cade said, tossing down his shoes and taking a seat next to her.

"I didn't plan to come. I just sort of started walking." Erica wanted to tell him to go away, but he had as much right to the beach as she did. She had nothing to say to him, though, so she pushed herself up to standing and dusted the sand off the back of her dress.

She wasn't giving up on her promotion, but she didn't have to be alone with Cade. As soon as she got back to the office, she'd clear Pauline's schedule for the next two weeks.

"Erica, wait," Cade said, reaching for her hand.

"What?" She snatched her hand back like his touch might burn her. "You were right upstairs, alright? I do need this gig. I need it to be a success. I'm just not sure how to do that when the client is… you. Any chance Jillian's coming back soon?"

"Considering her mom's in critical condition after a car crash, no, she isn't."

"Oh," Erica said, feeling stupid for asking, even though she had no way of knowing the situation. "Is she going to be okay?"

"Jury's still out. Jillian's flying back to New Jersey to be with her."

"Sorry." Erica wasn't sure what else to say.

"Can I ask you a question?" Cade's eyes met hers as he leaned back on his hands.

"I guess so." She shifted her bag to her other shoulder and twisted her feet so they dug a little further into the sand.

"Do you regret breaking up with me?"

"What?" Erica must have heard him wrong.

"Do you regret breaking up with me?" Cade sat up a little straighter and dusted the sand off his hands.

"Cade, what are you talking about? I stood right here, in this very spot, and listened to you tell me we were done."

Erica remembered that entire night as if it was yesterday. She'd been packing for college when he arrived to pick her up. They'd gone to their favorite burger spot and played mini-golf. As usual, they'd eventually ended up on the beach. When they reached the palm tree that marked their place, Cade pulled on Erica's hand so she faced him. She leaned in and pressed her lips against his. Cade wrapped his arms around her and kissed her back, but eventually broke away with a groan. "Erica, we need to talk."

Of everything she thought he might say, those five words were close to last on the list. Their relationship was rock solid. They were heading off to college together in a few weeks.

Numbly, she grabbed two corners of the blanket Cade carried under his arm and helped him spread it across the sand.

"I got into Columbia. The letter came last week." Cade remained standing instead of following her down onto the blanket.

"But you were wait-listed, and you're already set to go to USF. We leave in less than three weeks." Erica's mind spun. Surely, he wasn't changing plans now.

"I guess someone else dropped off last minute, and they offered me the spot."

"You aren't taking it, though, right?" Erica asked, even though she knew the answer already. He was leaving her.

He left *her*.

So why was he standing here now, ten years later, saying she'd been the one to end it?

"Erica, I stood here and told you I was going to Columbia, not that I wanted to break up with you. You're the one who refused to talk to me all the way home and then stopped taking my phone calls."

"But we had it all planned out." Erica felt an uncomfortable prickling as her whole body turned cold, then hot. What he said couldn't be true, could it? She *had* refused his calls, but only because it seemed pointless to drag things out. He was leaving. What was there to say?

"And if I could have stuck to that plan, I would've. My parents didn't give me much of a choice. They said it was Columbia, or they were cutting me off. I was eighteen, Erica. I didn't have a way to support myself, much less pay for school. I didn't have a scholarship to USF like you did," he said.

"You broke my heart that day!" Erica sank down on the sand where she stood. She sat a couple feet away from Cade, but the distance between them had never felt farther.

"And you broke mine every day afterward by refusing to pick up the phone or answer my emails!" His voice was thick with emotion. A single tear slid down his cheek, but he made no attempt to wipe it away.

Erica looked down at her hands, grasping at the grains of sand next to her like a lifeline. What was he saying? That they might still be together if she just talked to him afterward? Had she really been the one to end them? Aloud, she asked, "Do you really think we would've made it long distance?"

"I don't know. But you're the one who refused to try. You weren't just my girlfriend, Erica, you were my best friend. And just like every other best friend I ever had, you dropped out of my life the minute my parents pulled me out of your daily orbit. I needed you, and you weren't there." Cade's words hit her like stones.

"I needed you, too," Erica admitted, pulling her knees to her chest as tears began to fall again. "Sometimes it feels like I still do."

Cade closed the distance between them and wrapped his arms around her. She rested her cheek against his and allowed herself to relax into his embrace. He was more solid than he'd been in high school, his stubble scratchier against her face, but he still smelled the same—like citrus and bergamot.

She wasn't sure how long they sat like that, listening to the waves crash onto the sand. It felt right, being in his arms again. As long as they clung to each other, everything that might have been between them seemed possible. But as soon as she let go, the last ten years would swoop back in, and it would all disappear.

The sun was low on the horizon when she finally pulled back to look at him. His eyes were full of sadness, but she thought she saw a glimmer of hope, too. "So, where do we go from here?"

"How about a do-over?" Cade took her hand. This time, she let him, enjoying the feel of his skin against hers, the familiar sensation of butterflies when he brushed his thumb against her palm.

"I don't know where to find a time machine." Erica joked, though it came out sounding more sad than funny.

"No, but we could do burgers and mini-golf."

"They tore our mini-golf spot down a few years ago. Hurricane damage," she said.

"I'm sure we can find another place to play."

"Do you really think this is a good idea?"

Cade's mouth turned up into an almost-smile as he stood.

"Maybe." He reached down to help Erica up. "All I know is, we have to work together for the next two weeks, and we're not eighteen anymore. I think we owe it to ourselves—and this New Year's party—to stop living in the past and get to know each other as we are now."

CHAPTER 9

Cade drummed his fingers on the steering wheel of his black Jeep as he navigated the off ramp toward Erica's condo. This date was such a bad idea. The more he thought about it, the less forgiving he felt about their previous breakup. Even if Erica thought he'd wanted to end things, one answered phone call would have straightened things out. Was he willing to start over with someone who just stopped communicating at the first sign of trouble? Walking down memory lane with Erica seemed like a surefire way to get his heart broken again.

Cade almost wished he hadn't suggested it—almost, but not quite. It felt so right having her in his arms again on the beach two days ago. Erica had always been it for him, and if life was giving them a second chance, he knew he had to take it.

He flicked his left blinker on and waited for traffic to clear so he could turn into the small parking lot outside Erica's condo building. He pulled into a parking space, put the car in park, then texted to say he was there.

It was a little weird not to go to her door—Erica's mom had read him the riot act when he arrived for their first date and hit the horn. But Erica didn't live with her parents now, and it seemed pointless for her to buzz him up, only for them to leave as soon as he got to her door.

He waited only seconds before his phone vibrated.

Erica:
Be right down

Through his open window, he watched a young woman in a yellow sundress get out of her car and grab two grocery bags from the trunk. He decided she was headed to her boyfriend's place to make dinner. A harried-looking woman and two small kids spilled out of a minivan—on their way to visit Grandma, he mused. A couple walked hand in hand out the front door of Erica's building, each carrying a wrapped gift—definitely headed to an early Christmas party. Erica walked out next. She wore crop jeans, a long cardigan, and a genuine smile. Cade's heart squeezed at the sight.

"Hey," Erica said as she opened the passenger door and got in. He glanced at the clock on the dashboard and smirked when he saw it was seven o'clock on the dot.

Her mom always used to tell him she'd be ready on time, and not a minute sooner.

That hadn't changed, at least.

"Hey." Cade's heart pounded a little faster at having her so near.

"Hey," Erica smiled. "You're still driving a black Jeep."

The corners of his mouth turned up in a sheepish grin. He hadn't driven one since he lived here last, but when Jillian asked him what kind of car he wanted to lease from the dealership in Tampa, he instantly told her a black Jeep. Maybe somewhere deep down, he'd been hoping for a chance to relive the past.

"Bayside Grille for burgers?" He started the Jeep and put it in drive.

Erica laughed. "I haven't been there in forever, but sure, let's try it."

Cade tried to figure out what to say as he pulled out of the parking lot and headed toward the restaurant. Somehow all the usual date conversation topics seemed wrong, but so did the questions he'd ask when catching up with an old friend. Things used to be so easy between them. He wondered if they'd ever get that back.

"The radio spot today netted quite a few more ticket sales. I think we've sold seventy-five percent at this point." Erica took the easy option and opened with work. He guessed it was better than sitting in silence.

"That's great!" He was thrilled they were getting closer to selling out.

Out of the corner of his eye, he noticed Erica twisting her necklace. He caught the glint of a gold bow at the end of the chain. Was that—?

He cut off his own thought.

It couldn't be. No way. There was no way she still had the necklace he gave her for Christmas ten years ago.

He'd been so excited to give it to her. They'd been together for just over a year, and despite being barely eighteen, he was sure Erica was the girl he'd marry. He wanted to get her something perfect, something she'd love. In the end, his mom helped him choose a small gold bow that hung from a delicate gold chain. Erica's eyes lit up when she opened the small green and gold box, and she wore it almost every day for the rest of the school year.

If he wasn't mistaken, she was also wearing it now. After rolling to a stop at the next traffic light, he turned his head for a closer look. It was definitely his necklace.

"You still have it," He said, knowing he shouldn't read too much into it. But it meant something that she hadn't gotten rid of his gift.

"Huh?" Erica gave him a questioning look.

"That necklace."

"Oh," she glanced down at the little bow. "Yeah. It's so pretty, I could never bring myself to give it up." She tucked a strand of hair behind her ear and smiled shyly. "I still wear it sometimes, especially this time of year." She ducked her head as though it was something to be ashamed of.

Learning she still wore his necklace all these years later made his chest swell. She wasn't over him, either.

He reached over and casually took her hand in his. He half expected her to snatch it back, but was glad when she didn't.

"That was a great Christmas. Remember when I convinced you to help me decorate Christmas cookies?" Erica said, laughing.

"How could I forget?" Cade laughed too, remembering how he'd somehow turned his snowman cookie into a something out of a horror movie. Erica couldn't stop laughing, so of course, he kept making his cookies look weird.

"Your mom was so mad when she came home from her book club the next day," he said.

"It was her own fault for not looking at them before she grabbed them off the counter!" Erica giggled.

They spent the rest of the drive reminiscing about that

holiday break. Everything was so simple back then. Could they really get that back?

His body thought so, at least. Familiar sparks raced up his arm, starting where his palm pressed against hers, filling him with a combination of desire and contentment. He'd never experienced that chemistry with anyone else. After ten years without her, he'd almost convinced himself that he imagined it, but here it was, real.

A voice in the back of his head told him he was getting in too deep, too fast. That Erica would just hurt him again. But he pushed it aside. He'd been in love with her since he was seventeen years old, and even if this reunion was only temporary, he'd make the most of it.

He regretfully released her hand so they could get out of the car at the restaurant. He half-hoped she'd take his hand again as they walked toward the Grille, but she didn't. When they reached the door, he quickly stepped up to hold it open for her.

"Take a seat anywhere," the hostess said as they approached the stand.

There were several tables open. Cade followed Erica's lead to the third booth on the left wall of the restaurant. Erica slid into one side of the booth and he resisted the urge to sit next to her. It was cute when they did it as teenagers, but it would be obnoxious now.

Actually, it had probably been just as obnoxious when they were eighteen. But they were in their own little bubble back then, oblivious to everyone else when they were together.

He sat across from Erica and picked up the menu.

"I see they're still serving the burger with peanut butter." Erica scrunched up her face in disgust.

The menu had ten different burgers, and back when this was their regular date spot, Cade committed to trying them all. Erica had been so grossed out by the peanut butter bacon burger, he only ordered it the once.

"As I recall, it wasn't that bad. Maybe that's what I'll have tonight," said Cade, hoping to get a rise out of her.

"Not if you plan on kissing me," Erica said, making Cade's eyes go wide.

"So kissing's on the table if I don't get the peanut butter bacon burger?" He grinned.

Erica's face flushed red. "Oh, no. I didn't mean that." She shifted in her seat. "I mean, I'm sorry. For a second, we were back in high school. It just popped out."

"I know the feeling," Cade said, as the gulf of those ten years expanded between them again. At least now he knew it was happening to her, too.

When the waitress came over, Cade ordered a regular cheeseburger with lettuce and tomato. He skipped the onion, because despite Erica's embarrassment at bringing it up, he hoped to kiss her before the night was over. He added a milkshake to his order for old time's sake. Erica went with a Diet Coke to go with her veggie burger.

"How are your parents?" Cade asked while they waited for their food.

"They're good! Mom's busy with the foundation this time of year, and Dad's still working at the law firm. We're all heading up to my grandma's in Savannah for Christmas— just the 24th through the 26th, though, so it won't impact your event."

"I'm not worried. I've never known you to drop the ball on anything." She'd been pulling off large-scale parties since she chaired the high school dance committee. Cade was just glad he wouldn't have to go the entire week without seeing her.

Erica smiled at that. "What about yours? How's working with your dad?"

"Good, actually." Cade's relationship with his dad had been a little rocky back when he was dating Erica. His dad wanted him to apply himself more, and Cade just wanted to enjoy being a kid.

Cade would never admit it out loud, but breaking up with Erica had a positive impact on his grades when he got to Columbia. Still nursing a broken heart, he didn't have it in him to pour energy into building new relationships—even the non-romantic kind.

"I got straight A's my first semester, and my dad took that as a sign I was ready to get serious about my future. We worked pretty closely together the following summer, and he's been passing me more and more responsibility ever since," he said.

"That's really great, Cade," Erica said, as the waitress brought their food.

"Actually, you'll probably see my mom and dad around the hotel next week. They fly in tomorrow night." Cade reached for his cheeseburger and took a bite.

"They're spending Christmas here, then?" Erica nibbled on an extra-crispy fry. The action made him focus on her lips, which made him think about kissing her again.

"Yeah, they'll be here through New Year's."

"So I take it they'll be at the event?" Erica picked up her drink and wrapped her pink lips around the straw.

Cade shifted in his seat, his arms itching to wrap themselves around her. A part of him wished he'd taken the seat next to her after all.

"They'll be there," Cade confirmed, taking another bite of his food.

"No pressure or anything, having your dad there," Erica said, fiddling with her necklace. "Maybe we should skip mini-golf. I still have a lot of work ahead of me to make sure New Year's is perfect."

"No way." Cade wasn't about to let her end the night early. "Sounds like someone's just scared of ending her reign as mini-golf champ."

"Absolutely not." Erica said, making him grin. He knew her competitive nature wouldn't let her resist that taunt. "I hope you've been practicing, Cade Whitmore, otherwise you won't stand a chance."

CHAPTER 10

Erica concentrated on the bright pink golf ball as she lined up her club to tap it into the waiting hole. She was down by four. If she made this shot, it would only be three. Playing a weekly game of mini-golf with her friends should have given her an advantage, but this was a whole different course with different obstacles, and Cade was making it his mission to distract her.

She hit the ball and watched it roll slowly toward the hole, stopping just short of the edge.

"No!" she cried.

Cade laughed as she tipped the ball in with her club.

"Three," she grumbled, reaching in the hole and picking up both their balls.

He brushed his thumb against hers as she handed him his yellow ball, sending a shiver down her spine.

"You're distracting me on purpose!"

"I have no idea what you're talking about. I just took my ball out of your hand." Cade smirked as he wrote both their scores.

He knew *exactly* what he was doing. Still, it was hard to accuse him of cheating when the real problem was how her body reacted to his nearness. If she was honest, she'd been thinking about kissing him since she accidentally brought it up at dinner. She wished she hadn't been so awkward about it after. Then maybe he'd have kissed her already, and this electric tension between them wouldn't be so strong.

Cade dropped his ball on the black mat at the start of the next hole. He swung his putter. Erica watched in disbelief as the ball rolled straight between the three wooden posts and plunked down into the hole.

"Hole in one!" Cade shouted. He dropped his club and picked her up, spinning her around in celebration.

"Cade!" Erica laughed as she tried to ignore the heat that sprang from his hands where they touched her sides.

He set her down and tucked a strand of hair behind her ear, just like he always used to. Erica's heart beat faster as the tension between them became even more palpable. Her eyes locked on his, and she saw a mixture of hope and desire in them. She wondered if he saw those same things reflected back in hers.

As desperate as she was to close the distance between them and feel his lips moving against hers, she hesitated. Once she kissed him, there'd be no going back for her. She'd be handing him her heart, and despite everything she was feeling right now, she wasn't sure she could trust him with it again.

The sounds of a family playing the hole behind them broke the moment. "We should keep playing so they don't have to wait for us," Erica said, stepping back from Cade.

He moved to the side so she could take her swing.

Though they were no longer touching, she still felt the electricity sparking between them.

She took her swing. The ball followed almost the same path as his had, but skirted the rim of the hole instead of dropping in.

"Robbed!" she yelled, walking up to tap her ball into the hole alongside Cade's.

Cade's breath tickled her ear as he stepped behind her and whispered, "Nice shot."

She shivered, though the night was anything but cold.

"Cade?" she whispered.

"Hmm?" He stepped closer, pressing his chest to her back.

"You and me. Is this for real, or are we just holding onto old chemistry?"

He wrapped an arm around her and grabbed her free hand, twirling her so she faced him. "I've never met anyone else who makes me feel the way I feel when I'm with you. If this isn't real, I don't know what is."

Erica dropped the club she was still holding. This time, she didn't hesitate. Cade's club clattered to the ground next to hers as he met her halfway. Their lips finally connected, sending fireworks straight to her core.

She wrapped her arms around his waist, pulling him closer. His hand cupped the back of her neck as he swept his tongue past her lips, deepening the kiss. She stood up on her tiptoes and kissed him back with everything she had.

The ten years they spent apart seemed to melt away as she lost herself in him. They were getting a second chance, and she'd be crazy not to take it.

CHAPTER 11

Erica was still floating on air the next day when she walked into the office. Instead of finishing their round of mini-golf, she and Cade drove to their spot on the beach and made out like teenagers. Eventually, they'd have to talk about the logistics of their relationship, but for now, Erica was just happy to have the man she loved back in her life.

"Erica, got a minute?" Harrison called as she passed his office on her way to grab a cup of coffee from the kitchenette.

"What's up?" She hovered in his doorway, wishing he'd caught her *after* she had her coffee. Hopefully, this would be quick.

He motioned for her to take a seat. So much for getting out of here fast.

"Just wanted to check how the New Year's event at the Calix is coming along. Any concerns I should be aware of?"

"We're obviously working within a tight timeline, but we're in a good spot. No major concerns." Erica was proud of what she'd put together in the last three weeks. There was still a lot of work to do, but she had no doubt the party would be a success. Especially now that she and Cade were on good terms.

"Really? Because Pauline mentioned there are still over thirty tickets available. It's the Friday before Christmas, and *I'm* concerned we're not sold out yet." Harrison made a tent with his fingers and leaned in. "What's your plan?"

Crap. Erica's plan had been to grab a coffee and figure that out. She couldn't remember the last time she'd stayed out so late on a work night. Not that she'd change anything about her date with Cade.

"It's only been three weeks. A hundred and twenty-five tickets is a lot to sell in that amount of time."

Harrison sighed and gave her a disappointed look. "I interviewed someone for the Director of Events position this morning. When I asked him what he'd do in this situation, he had an excellent answer."

"Wait, you're still interviewing?" Erica knew she was on trial here, but if Harrison was still talking to other candidates, it meant he wasn't sold on promoting her.

"I told you I'd give you a shot—and I am—but to be honest, I'm worried it's too much pressure. Don't think I haven't noticed you dragging Pauline to all your on-site meetings." Harrison's words hit her like a bucket of ice water.

"You're the one always telling me I need to delegate more." Erica said.

Great. Instead of arguing her case, she'd just reminded Harrison of her biggest weakness. She blamed the lack of sleep and coffee.

"It's not delegating unless it makes less work for you. That's a lesson you'll need to learn quickly if you want to run the department."

Erica swallowed against the hard lump that formed in her throat.

"And what happened to you on Tuesday afternoon? We were expecting you to give an update at the four o'clock meeting, but you didn't show. Luckily, Pauline stepped up to cover." Harrison pointed out yet another mistake.

See, that's delegation, Erica wanted to say, but knew it wouldn't help her case. Neither would the truth, that she'd been on the beach with Cade, and work had been the furthest thing from her mind.

She couldn't remember another time in her career when she'd just no-showed to a meeting, but she didn't regret her choice. If she hadn't gone to the beach, she and Cade wouldn't have talked. They wouldn't be back together now.

Harrison was waiting for a response, so she went with the almost-truth. "I'm really sorry about Tuesday. The client showed up really late for the tasting, then wanted to talk to me after."

"You know I love working with you, Erica, but I have serious concerns about your ability to take over the Events department. I'm sorry, but from what I've seen these last three weeks, you're just not ready."

Panic welled up inside her as she tried to figure out what might compel him to give her another chance.

Seeing Cade again had thrown her for a loop, but everything was great now. The event was on track. The DJ and photo booth were all set to go. Food was handled. Decorations were going to be minimal, but she'd ordered what they needed last week. She'd only started advertising this party a week and a half ago, and had already sold ninety-five tickets.

She had this.

He couldn't not give her the promotion if the party went

well, could he? The thought of failing now, when she was so close to pulling this off, was almost too much to bear.

"So that's it, then? You're not even going to let me finish out this event?"

Harrison didn't answer right away, and Erica felt her armpits dampen while she waited for him to speak.

"We made a deal, and I'll honor it. But you'll have to make some major strides in a short time to have me change my mind. And I expect to see a sold out event by Monday."

Erica sat at her desk a few hours later, racking her brain for a good way to sell the last thirty tickets by Monday. She was on her second coffee, this one a peppermint mocha, courtesy of Pauline. Even sufficiently caffeinated, she wasn't coming up with any answers. She wanted to ask Harrison what the other candidate's brilliant idea was, but that would mean admitting the other guy knew something she didn't—which wasn't an option.

Her phone vibrated with an incoming text. Despite her current predicament, she smiled when she saw Cade's name on the screen.

Cade:
What are you up to this afternoon? Our bartender is giving me a preview of our signature New Year's drinks. Want to join?

She chewed her lip, considering. She still had a lot of work to do, but couldn't resist the opportunity to spend time with Cade.

Erica:

I'd love to. What time are you thinking?
I'm not sure I can leave the office before 5.

She didn't want Harrison thinking she was ducking out
early.

Cade:

*Even for a client? *winking emoji**

Erica supposed it *was* event-related, but that didn't erase
the number of things on her to-do list. She couldn't leave
anything to chance with this event. The promotion wasn't
the only thing raising the stakes. Cade's dad would be there,
and she couldn't help feeling like she had something to
prove. Calvin Whitmore never made it a secret that he didn't
approve of how serious Cade and Erica were back in high
school. Cade told her all the time that it wasn't personal, but
that didn't stop her from wanting to impress him.

Erica:

4:30? I have a lot to get done today...for a client that decided to
throw a NYE bash with only 4 weeks notice.

She didn't have to wait long for his response.

Cade:

Wow, who would do that?

Erica grinned, loving their easy banter.

Cade:

I guess I'll survive until then. Actually, that gives me time to meet with the hotel's lead accountant. Thank goodness I have people for that. I was never good at debits and credits.

Erica doubted Cade was as bad at accounting as he said, but it made her realize something. Selling the remaining tickets wasn't all on her—she had people, too.

Erica:

*See you at 4:30! *kissing-heart face emoji**

She set her phone down and got to work, sending an instant message to the designer assigned to the drink menus and calling an impromptu meeting for all available event planners and marketing strategists. She had a New Year's party to sell out, and as a future leader in this company, she was demanding all hands on deck.

Three hours later, she had a plan. It was far from foolproof, but it was the best she could expect from her team on the Friday before Christmas. As it stood, she'd had to bribe them with lunch from their favorite Mediterranean takeout spot, so they'd action it this afternoon.

Cade's goal was to generate buzz for the Calix Rooftop, so the plan was to give a handful of tickets away to local influencers. In exchange, the influencers would mention the party on their social media. Their posts would help to sell the rest of the tickets, and, any photos they shared from the event itself would give the hotel even more publicity.

Erica was on her final review of the completed drink menus when Pauline and Jack, another event coordinator, stopped by her desk.

"We're all going to head out soon to grab drinks with Madeline, since it's her last day. You almost done here?" said Pauline.

A hint of heartburn sprang up in Erica's chest. She was double-booked tonight. How had she let that happen? She sighed, trying to figure out how to be in two places at once. She didn't want to bail on Cade, but there was no way she could miss Madeline's last-day drinks.

"Did Madeline say where she wanted to go?" Erica asked, an idea taking shape in her mind.

"I think it's still TBD," Jack replied.

"What if we all did drinks at the Calix? The rooftop isn't open yet, but they have a really cool lobby bar. You guys can preview the New Year's drink specials with me."

"You don't think Jillian will mind? That's quite a few extra test drinks." Pauline raised her eyebrows.

"Let me ask." Erica didn't bother to clarify that she was asking Cade instead of Jillian. Though part of her wanted to scream it from the rooftop that she and Cade were back together, Pauline would want details, and this wasn't the place. The last thing she needed was for Harrison to learn her so-called screw-ups were because of a boy. She'd be deemed too emotional, and he'd give the job to that male candidate in a heartbeat.

Erica:

Hey. It's my current boss's last day and everyone wants to go out for drinks. Mind if I bring the crew with me to taste test?

Erica held her breath as she watched the gray dots appear, then disappear, then reappear on the bottom of her screen. It was a lot to ask, considering they'd only just gotten back together, but she didn't want to have to choose between him and her coworkers.

Cade:
Sure. One condition, though.

Erica:
What's that?

Cade:
You have to promise I get some alone time with you after they leave.

Erica:
Deal

She smiled as she sent the menus off to the printer. Given how badly her day started, she was pleased with how it turned out. Not only would she get to see Cade while celebrating Madeline, but bringing everyone to the hotel would show them just how under control Erica had this event.

CHAPTER 12

"Hey Dad," Cade answered his phone as he strode through the hotel lobby on his way to meet Erica. The bar was busier than usual, making him glad he'd reserved a section for Erica's team. His parents were supposed to fly in later tonight, and he hoped his dad wasn't calling to tell him they were delayed.

"Hey Cade, just calling to let you know we'll be there in around fifteen minutes." His dad said through the phone. "Do you have plans for dinner?"

"Wait, what?" Cade stopped walking. He thought they were coming in later tonight, but he was a lot less organized than usual after being without Jillian for a few days.

"I finished early at the office, so we grabbed an earlier flight. It was a last-minute decision," said his dad.

A phone call before they boarded would've been nice. Cade was excited to see his parents, but he also wanted to spend time with Erica, and he wasn't quite ready to mash the two together yet.

"I still have a couple more meetings, but could do a late

dinner." Cade wasn't sure what his parents would think of his reunion with Erica, but he'd prefer to find out later tonight when he had them alone. The last thing he wanted was for them to scare her off, especially if they weren't immediately thrilled about his seeing her again.

"Great, that'll give us time to get settled," said his dad. "Does eight o'clock work?"

"Works for me. Does anything in particular sound good?" Cade glanced at his watch. Erica would arrive any minute, and so would his parents.

"Your mom's been talking about fresh grouper all day. Think your assistant could make us a reservation somewhere with good seafood?"

Once again, Cade missed Jillian. She was more than his assistant, she was his right hand, and running this place was a heck of a lot harder without her. "Jillian's actually out of town, but I'll ask the concierge to make one."

After hanging up with his dad, Cade texted Erica to say he was running a little late, but had reserved a table for her. Selfishly, he hoped her work friends wouldn't hang around for too long. He wanted her to himself for a while before dinner with his parents. Even though he saw her less than twenty-four hours ago, he couldn't wait to have her in his arms again.

At the host stand, he ordered a couple bottles of champagne for Erica's group—on the house, of course. That taken care of, he headed to the front desk to warn them his parents were on their way. His parents weren't particularly demanding hotel guests, but he'd learned long ago that employees always appreciated a heads up when the CEO of the hotel was about to walk in.

He'd just asked the concierge about dinner when a

familiar prickle told him Erica was near. Hearing her laugh echo across the lobby confirmed she'd arrived. He wanted to run over, spin her around, and kiss her senseless—but thought better of it when he saw his parents push through the revolving door behind her. He gave her a casual wave instead.

She smiled and gave a little wave back.

Cade breathed a sigh of relief when she turned and led her coworkers to the lobby bar, but it was short-lived. She said something to the host, waved her group on without her, and doubled back toward Cade. Quickening her pace, she gave him a wide smile. Over her shoulder, he saw his parents were headed his way, too. Despite his misgivings about their unavoidable meeting, he couldn't help but return Erica's grin.

"Hey Mom!" Cade called out, wanting Erica to know his parents were there before she moved into hugging range.

Erica looked confused for a second, then glanced over her shoulder.

"Cade!" His mom stepped around Erica and wrapped him in a hug, then moved back so that his dad could do the same.

Erica stood awkwardly to the side as Cade shared a brief hug with his dad. She looked unsure whether she should join the greeting or walk away.

"Erica?" His mom noticed her, taking away the choice.

"Hi, Mrs. Whitmore. Uh, Cade didn't mention you were coming in today."

"We hopped on an earlier flight and surprised him," his mom told her. She looked back and forth between Cade and Erica, as though she was waiting for one of them to explain why Erica was here.

"Mom, Dad, Erica's company is helping us pull off the

New Year's event. They've done a great job so far," Cade said, purposely avoiding any mention of their personal relationship.

"Great! I look forward to attending." Cade's dad looked at Erica. "Did you two have a meeting now, or—?"

"We do," Cade interjected. "But I can spare a few minutes to get you and mom settled. Erica, if you want to head over to the bar, I'll meet you shortly."

He saw a flicker of hurt cross Erica's face at the casual dismissal. He opened his mouth to fix it, but the icy mask had already settled over her face.

"Sure, I'll see you soon. Nice seeing you again, Mr. and Mrs. Whitmore."

She strode away with her chin up and her back ramrod straight. That body language might project confidence to everyone else, but he knew it was a shield to cover how she felt inside. Knowing how pissed off she was didn't stop him from appreciating how good her backside looked in that skirt, but it did make him wonder how hard it would be to get back in her good graces. His entire goal had been to avoid upsetting her. He knew she'd have a hard time enjoying drinks with her colleagues if his parents reacted badly to their getting back together. Yet somehow, he'd managed to offend her all on his own.

"I didn't expect to see *her* here," His mom said when Erica was out of earshot.

Cade dragged his gaze away from his girlfriend's retreating form.

"Yeah, it was a pretty big surprise for me, too." So much had changed since that first meeting. He could hardly believe it had only been three weeks. "But she's done a great job with the event."

"The hotel looks wonderful, Cade. I'm impressed at how you were able to transform the lobby without major renovations." As usual, his dad's thoughts didn't stray from the Calix Collection for long.

"Thanks," he said, grateful for the change in subject. He was proud of the lobby, and was thrilled to hear his dad liked it, too.

"The only thing I might change is moving the concierge desk to the other side. Might improve the flow." There it was. Cade loved his dad, but the man always had an opinion and never failed to let him know what it was.

"Sure. We're pretty full for the holidays, but I'll work on switching it as soon as the rush is over." Cade thought the concierge desk was fine where it was, but when it came to the hotel, it was easier to just say 'yes' than to try to change his dad's mind. Besides, Cade was saving his persuasion skills for Erica.

CHAPTER 13

Erica slid onto the bench seat next to Pauline, still reeling from the brief encounter with Cade's parents. She thought she and Cade were on the same page about their relationship—that they were back together—but clearly, she'd been mistaken. He dismissed her like she was any other business contact. It was obvious he didn't want to tell his parents they were back together, except that didn't make sense. They'd find out eventually—unless Cade didn't see this as a long-term thing. Erica's chest tightened. Was she just the latest in his string of casual hook-ups?

"When did you have time to arrange this?" Pauline gestured at the reserved tables and waiting champagne.

Caroline, another event manager, and Kate, Erica's favorite designer, leaned in across the table. They were obviously curious how she pulled this off as well. With a glance down the row of tables where Jack and Madeline sat with the rest of their colleagues, Erica had to admit Cade really came through. She'd be a lot more impressed he hadn't just brushed her off in front of his parents, though.

Erica pasted on a smile and pushed the encounter with Cade to the back of her mind. She was here to give Madeline a fun send-off, and that's what she'd to do. She could harp on her relationship with Cade later.

"I just said I was bringing a few more people." Erica said. "I guess they wanted to thank us for our work on the New Year's party."

"Based on the flurry of activity in the conference room today, I figured you had a huge fire to put out." Caroline grinned. "I should've known you had it all under control."

"The event is on track." Erica twirled a piece of hair between her fingers. "There was just a lot to tackle before we left for the holidays." *Not to mention the added pressure from Harrison to sell out by Monday.*

"Thanks for arranging all this, Erica." Madeline slid in on her right. "I know it's not official, but I think you're going to make a great department head."

"I'm just glad we could send you off in style," Erica accepted a glass of champagne from Pauline. "And thanks, but I'm not so sure Harrison's convinced."

"He'll give it to you. He's just making you work for it." Madeline sipped her champagne.

"Here's hoping." Erica picked up her glass and gave Madeline's a clink, wondering where Harrison was. Surely, seeing this would help her case.

"Remember that time Madeline reallocated the breakfast budget to a cocktail hour for that women's conference but forgot to update the web team, so the app said there was breakfast, and we had a hoard of hangry ladies waiting for food on the first day?" Caroline said, making everyone, including Madeline, laugh.

It was one of the few times Erica ever saw Madeline

screw up in a client-facing way, and the team gave her a hard time about it for months. Eventually, it became a running joke, with the two or three women who politely asked about breakfast becoming a screaming hoard in the retelling.

"It was not an angry hoard," Madeline said indignantly. "It was only a couple of ladies. Erica came back with bagels and pastries before most people even noticed."

"And then we got chewed out by the hotel for bringing in outside food," Erica remembered. Their contact at the hotel threatened to bill them for breakfast, since it was against policy to bring other food in.

"And Erica told them they could either be good sports about it or lose the conference to another hotel the following year, even though we had no say in where that group held their events," Madeline said. "I'm sad I won't be seeing you guys all the time, but I am glad I created an opportunity for Erica to lead. You're lucky to have her in charge!"

Erica flushed. Normally she'd appreciate the compliment, but the very public acknowledgment that she was being considered for Madeline's job meant it would be even worse if Harrison gave it to someone else.

Despite being hurt by the way he acted earlier, Erica was glad when Cade walked up. At least it pulled the attention off of her.

"Everyone, this is Cade Whitmore. His family owns the Calix Collection, and he's in charge of operations here." Erica went around the table, introducing all her colleagues. If he wanted to act like they were just two people working on an event together, she'd do the same. Cade took the open seat kitty-corner from her as two waiters passed out samples of three different cocktails.

"Thanks so much for all you've done to make our last-minute New Year's party a success." Cade said, looking straight at Erica as he held up a glass of yellowish liquid.

"Which of these is which?" asked Kate.

"The blue one's the midnight martini. It'll be served in a martini glass with a lemon twist. This one," the waiter pointed to the drink Cade was holding, "is the Lemon Ball Drop. The dark one is the Out with the Old Fashioned."

They all picked up a yellow drink and held up their glasses. Erica was surprised Cade selected this one to try first. It looked the least appetizing of the three.

She took a tentative sip, then fought not to spit it back out as the offensive flavor coated her taste buds. She'd never tasted Lemon Pine-Sol before, but she suspected the bartender might've tossed some in. With a grimace, she forced herself to swallow the concoction instead of spitting it across the table.

"What's in this?" Madeline sputtered out, her eyes watering at the horrible taste. The rest of the group had a similar reaction.

"No idea," said the waiter. "But I'm surprised you let Jason make you anything original. You know he doesn't drink, right?"

A look of embarrassed surprise flitted across Cade's face. Erica almost felt sorry for him, but she was still mad about how he treated her earlier. Maybe this was karma.

"They can't all be bad," Cade said with a forced grin. "Let's try the next one."

Erica picked up the amber-colored drink and gave herself a silent pep as she brought it to her nose for a sniff. She wanted to tell Cade he was on his own trying this one, but he was a client, and her entire team was watching. Her nose wrinkled as she brought the glass to her lips. On the bright side, it tasted better than the first one—but only because the Ball Drop was so terrible it was hard to compete.

"That's better, but still horrible," said Pauline. Erica eyed the blueish liquid of the last drink warily. She didn't need to taste it to know it was going to be gross. People were going to complain about these drinks.

"I don't know," Jack said, holding up the glass and squinting at it as he swirled the liquid around. "I could at least finish this one."

"Please, don't," Cade said. "Order whatever you want. This next round is on me. We'll… get these fixed by New Year's."

"Good thing we didn't list the ingredients on the menus!" Kate said cheerfully. Erica pushed to have them, but Kate insisted the design was better if they left them off.

"Yeah, good thing," Erica mumbled, wishing she hadn't brought the team here to do this. It was supposed to be a fun way to send Madeline off, but the whole evening was turning into a disaster. It wasn't just the drinks, either. She wasn't sure how long she could sit across from Cade, acting like everything was fine.

"I'll be back in a few." She headed to the restroom, planning to make an excuse to leave as soon as she got back. After the way Cade dismissed her earlier, she had no intention of spending extra time with him tonight.

As she exited the restroom, a hand caught her wrist and pulled her further into the dimly lit hallway.

"Ahh," she yelped as she fell into a pair of familiar arms. "I'm not in the mood to play this game, Cade." She pushed him away.

"Wait! Erica, I know you're mad at me, but I can explain."

Cade's grip on her wrist loosened, but the earnest look in his eyes held her in place.

"What are we doing here, Cade? I thought we were back together."

"We are."

"Then why did you brush me off like the hired help when your parents showed up?" Erica bit her lip. Cade seemed sincere, but if he was serious about her, were his parents the problem? Maybe they didn't think she was good enough for their son.

"If I told them we were back together, they'd want to hang around and talk, and you'd feel obligated to stay. I knew your work friends were waiting so…." Cade trailed off.

As explanations went, his was pretty solid. Erica searched his eyes for any sign that he wasn't being totally honest with her, but found only genuine concern.

She sighed. "Sorry for overreacting."

"It's okay. I knew as soon as I said it that it came out wrong." Cade brushed a strand of hair behind her ear. "And just for the record, I'm planning to tell them about us at dinner tonight. Now can I kiss you?"

Erica stood on her tiptoes and brought her lips to his in answer. Cade's arms wrapped tightly around her, and the world faded away, like it always did when she was with him.

"Ahem!"

Erica jumped away from Cade and shot a panicked look down the hallway. She breathed a sigh of relief when she saw it was Pauline.

Erica would have some explaining to do, but at least Pauline knew her history with Cade. If it was anyone else from work, it would look like she was kissing a random client.

"I think I'll head back out there," Cade said, giving Erica's hand a squeeze before striding quickly out of the hallway.

As soon as he turned his back, Pauline fanned her hand next to her face. "I think I need to go splash some water on my face, because dang, that kiss was hot!"

Erica's face flamed. *Anyone* could've walked into this hallway and seen them kissing.

"By the way, Harrison just got here. He's looking for you. He did not seem happy when Kate and Caroline told him about the terrible drinks. I'd get out there, if I were you."

"Crap." It was bad enough that her boss had yet another event mishap to hold over her head. But what if it had been him who saw her kissing Cade? She doubted he considered making out with clients a good leadership trait. The agency didn't have an official policy against dating clients, but everyone knew it was a recipe for disaster—just look at how she and Cade struggled to work together at first, and their breakup was ten years old. She'd have to be more careful around her coworkers from now on. No one else could find out she was romantically involved with Cade, at least until after she got the promotion.

She turned to go face the music. The drinks thing wasn't actually her fault, but Harrison would make it her job to fix it. She took two steps down the hall before Pauline called after her.

"Don't think you're getting away without telling me how you went from avoiding Cade to... *that.*" She waved her hands to indicate the kiss.

"I promise I'll fill you in, but just keep it quiet, okay? He's a client, and the last thing I need is for everyone to know we're...you know..." Erica gestured toward the other end of the hallway.

"My lips are sealed," Pauline mimed zipping her lips closed. Erica hoped they stayed that way.

She trusted Pauline, but her friend tended to let things slip by accident. Fortunately for Erica, they wouldn't all be back in the office until after the event, so if she got through tonight, there'd be minimal opportunity for Pauline to spill the beans.

CHAPTER 14

A few hours later, Cade sat across from his parents at the waterfront restaurant. He took another bite of salad, listening to his parents' light-hearted argument over what had and hadn't changed in the last ten years. His mom thought this restaurant was new, and his dad thought it had just changed hands. Cade smiled and stayed out of it, knowing better than to choose a side, no matter how good-natured the disagreement was. It felt good to have dinner with his family—it made him realize how much he missed having them around.

"Speaking of things that haven't changed, I didn't expect to run into Erica at the hotel today." Cade's mom took a sip of her white wine and watched him closely. She'd know his true feelings just by looking at his face. Lucky for him, he had no reason to lie.

"It was a pretty big surprise when I learned Jillian hired the agency Erica works for, and *she* was the event planner assigned to us."

"And you just went along with it? That girl broke your

heart when she stopped talking to you. You couldn't find another agency? Or ask this one to give you another event planner?" His mom picked up her wine glass, then set it back down without taking a drink.

Cade shook his head. "They're the best agency around, and even if they weren't, we started so last minute we didn't have time to pull in another one."

"You could have just let Jillian handle the party." His dad pushed away the remains of his ahi tuna appetizer. "She's certainly being paid enough. I still don't understand why you insist on having someone so overqualified as your personal assistant, especially if you're not willing to use—"

"We've been over this, Dad," Cade said, not wanting to get into this argument again. When it came to the business, Cade usually just caved to his father's wishes. Jillian was the one thing Cade continued to stand his ground on.

"I insist on keeping Jillian so that I *can* hand things like this party off to her." Cade put up his hand to stop his dad from interrupting. "Which I did, until she found out her mom was in the hospital, and I told her to go be with her."

"Calvin, drop the Jillian thing," said his mom. "I'm not sitting through another dinner where the two of you keep on about it. She makes Cade's life easier. Let him have that."

She turned to Cade as the waitress cleared their starter plates. "How has it been, working with Erica?"

"Great, actually. Once we got over the awkward part. It turns out I wasn't the only one who went to college with a broken heart. She assumed my leaving for Columbia meant I was breaking up with her." Cade brought his water glass to his lips and took a deep gulp. Just thinking about all that time they missed together made his chest tighten.

His mom took in his expression. "Oh, honey!"

"It's okay, mom. This event gave us a second chance." Cade grinned. "We're seeing each other again."

"Really? How come you didn't say anything when we saw her at the hotel?" His mom took another sip of wine.

"She was meeting up with a bunch of coworkers, and I knew if I told you then, you'd have a million questions for her." Cade took a sip of his own wine.

"I would not!" his mom said, indignant.

Cade just cocked his head and raised his eyebrows.

"Well, of course I want to get reacquainted with the girl you're dating. It's not like you've brought anyone home since her."

"We'll set up dinner while you guys are here," Cade promised.

His dad opened his mouth to say something, but closed it when the waitress arrived carrying their main courses.

Cade waited until the waitress finished passing out their food. "You looked like you had something you wanted to say, Dad." He braced himself for whatever objection his father was about to make.

"I just hope this doesn't mean you're going to lose focus. You've been doing an excellent job with the hotels, but last time you fell head over heels for Erica, your grades suffered. And what happens when you're needed elsewhere? Is she going to refuse your calls again?"

"First off, my B+ average had nothing to do with Erica. I was a teenager, and my classes were boring. Second, this is still new and we haven't talked about it, but I'm here for at least another year. And besides, she wouldn't do that again, not when the first time hurt her as much as it did me." Cade didn't want to admit it, but his dad's second question picked at the wound Erica left on his heart all those years ago. It had healed over, but the scar was still there.

"Your dad's just telling you to be careful, Cade. Neither of us wants to see you broken-hearted again." His mom gave him a sympathetic look as she took a bite of her grouper.

Cade took a bite of his own fish, but found he could hardly get it past the lump in his throat that formed at the thought of losing Erica again. He swallowed, then took a big gulp of water. He understood his parent's concerns, but he and Erica were meant to be. Why else would fate have brought them together again all these years later?

"I'm sorry, Cade. We didn't mean to upset you." His mom must have read the emotions on his face.

"It's alright, mom. I get it. I don't want to have my heart broken again either. But it's not like I can just back out of this." He was already in too deep. "Erica's it for me. I'm not sure I ever stopped loving her."

CHAPTER 15

Erica slid into the backseat of her dad's BMW with a sigh of relief. The last few days were a blur of finalizing New Year's details and last-minute Christmas shopping. The latter was something she vowed she'd never do again. After fighting the crowds through picked-over stores, she understood why people like her friend Zack hated Christmas. It wasn't like her to wait until the last weekend, but between Cade and fighting for the promotion, the entire month of December got away from her. At least now she could relax for a few days.

"Glad you're joining us, Erica! I was worried you wouldn't be able to make it with how busy your job's been," her dad said as he started the car and pulled away from her apartment.

"Like I'd ever hear the end of it if I bowed out," Erica said with a grin. Her mom's parents lived in Savannah, GA, and ever since Erica was little, the entire extended family spent Christmas there. It was one of Erica's favorite traditions. Even though they were mostly grown up now, she still loved gathering around the tree with her cousins on Christmas morning.

"I thought you enjoyed going." Her mom gave her a concerned look.

"I was kidding, mom!" Erica laughed. "You know I'd never miss Christmas in Savannah, but it's also true that Grandma had a fit last year when Julia went to her boyfriend's instead."

"True. Speaking of boyfriends, how are things going with Cade?" asked her mom. Erica had filled her in over the phone last week after she and Cade got back together.

"They're good!" Erica wished they'd been able to spend a little more time together the last few days, but their schedules hadn't lined up for more than a brief lunch at the hotel. Supposedly, his parents were supportive when he talked to them. She hoped that was true, since they were taking her and Cade to dinner the day after she got back.

ERICA ROLLED over in the quilt-covered twin bed and breathed in the scent of Christmas—a mixture of coffee, cinnamon buns, and the fresh pine boughs her grandmother scattered through the house as Christmas decorations. She glanced over at her cousin, Julia, with whom she'd shared a room at family events for as long as she could remember.

Julia was still sound asleep, not that Erica could blame her. They'd stayed up late last night catching up. Erica filled Julia in on Cade and the promotion. Julia filled Erica in on the latest with her boyfriend, Brad. She'd been expecting a proposal before they left for their respective family Christmases and was bummed when Brad hadn't popped the question.

"There's always New Year's," Erica had said. In her opinion, a Christmas engagement was a cop-out. An engagement ring wasn't a Christmas gift. A New Year's proposal, on the other hand—that was romantic.

She let her mind wander to when and how Cade might ask her to marry him, not caring that the entire line of thinking was premature. She and Cade had barely been back together for a full week. A girl could dream, though.

As though he knew she was thinking of him, her phone buzzed on the nightstand next to her bed.

Cade:

Merry Christmas! Did Santa bring you anything special?

Erica:

Merry Christmas to you too. And not yet. I just woke up.

Cade:

It's 9AM. I thought you always got up super early for presents at your grandparents' house.

Erica shook her head, but a smile played across her lips. She couldn't believe he remembered that.

Erica:

We did when we were kids. Now that all the cousins are grown up, we sleep in and eat breakfast first.

Cade:

Is it bad that I miss you already? I can't wait to have you back in my arms.

Erica grinned. Even though she saw him two days ago, she missed him, too. Ever since their conversation on the beach, she wanted to spend every waking minute with him. It was good to know he felt the same.

Erica:
*I miss you, too. I can't wait to have my lips on yours. *kissing-heart face emoji**

Cade:
Now I'm going to be thinking of kissing you all through brunch with my parents.

Erica let out a partial laugh, then covered her mouth with her hands. She glanced over at her cousin, who rolled over with a groan.

Erica:
Have a great Christmas, Cade. Can't wait to see you when I get back.

She almost added *I love you,* but realized she hadn't told him that yet—at least, not since they got back together. Those words were a big deal to her, and she didn't want to say them for the first time via text.

Cade:
I can't wait, either. Have fun with your family, and tell your parents I said hi.

Erica:
Will do. Tell yours I said hi too.

She set her phone down and stretched, a smile on her face. She never expected to have Cade back in her life, but now that he was, she couldn't imagine the rest of it without him.

"Let me guess, that was Cade." Julia drew out the 'a' in Cade, using a sing-song voice.

Erica laughed and tossed a pillow at her.

"I just thought of something." Julia sat up in bed, hugging the pillow Erica just threw. "Cade's your client, right? Isn't dating him a conflict of interest with your promotion?"

Erica rubbed a hand down her face. "Don't remind me. But we only have to keep it quiet until after New Year's, and that's only a few days away."

"You don't think it'll call the promotion into question if you're suddenly dating the client it hinged on two days after you get it?" Julia set the pillow aside and slid out of bed. She walked over to her suitcase and rummaged through it until she found a sweatshirt to toss on over the cami she wore to bed.

Erica sat motionless as Julia's words sunk in. How hadn't she thought of that? Surely, Harrison wouldn't take the promotion away once he gave it to her, would he? A few weeks ago, she'd have said no, but after last Friday, she wasn't so sure. She thought failing to get the promotion was the worst thing that could happen, but having it taken away after she got it would be so much worse. How would she face her colleagues after that?

BACK FROM SAVANNAH, Erica could barely contain her excitement as she crossed the Calix lobby. She spotted Cade leaning against the wall near the elevator and increased her pace. It had only been a few days, but she couldn't wait to be near him again, even if she was a little nervous about having dinner with his parents.

"Hey," she breathed, coming to a stop in front of him.

"Hey." He smiled. Stepping forward, he wrapped her in a hug and leaned in for a kiss. Longing blossomed in her core as she linked her hands around his neck. Just as his lips were about to brush hers, her cousin's words echoed through her head, dousing her desire like an unexpected rain shower. *You don't think it'll call your promotion into question if you're suddenly dating the client?* She turned her head, so his lips landed on her cheek instead.

"What's wrong?" Cade asked, reaching out to cup her chin with his hand.

She shifted out of his grasp. "It's just…I don't think public displays of affection are such a good idea."

"What changed?" A look of hurt flashed across Cade's face. Her chest tightened, hating that she caused it.

"Nothing." She said, wanting to reassure him that her feelings stayed the same.

"It's not nothing, or you would've kissed me just now." Cade frowned. "Are you having second thoughts?"

"No. That's not it, I promise." Erica tucked a strand of hair behind her ear and played with the ends. "I want to be with you. It's just that my promotion hinges on this party, and I'm afraid it's going to look bad if I'm dating the client."

"Okay. I get that. But no one you work with is here right now." Cade closed the distance between them again.

Erica glanced around the lobby and saw he was right. Maybe she was being a little over-cautious. Hesitantly, she stepped into his arms and rested her face against his chest, breathing in his familiar scent. "I'm sorry. I'm just afraid to lose everything I worked so hard for, you know?"

"So you want to keep our relationship quiet until after New Year's?"

"It might have to be a little longer than that…just so, you know, it doesn't look like our relationship is the reason you give me a glowing review." Erica looked up at him with pleading eyes, hoping he'd understand.

He sighed and dropped a kiss on top of her head. "I just got you back, Er. I don't want to have to hide how I feel about you."

The elevator dinged and Cade's parents stepped out, effectively ending the conversation, though Erica was pretty sure it was anything but over.

CHAPTER 16

"That was actually really fun," Erica said, crossing her legs in the passenger seat of Cade's Jeep. "Think we could do Sunday brunch with my parents next weekend?"

"I'll have to double check my calendar, but I think that works." Cade gave her hand a squeeze as they pulled back into the hotel parking lot after a successful the dinner with his parents. His mom had greeted Erica with a huge hug, and apologized for the cool greeting the night they got in. It was obvious Erica was nervous at first, but she seemed to relax by the time they dug into their appetizers.

She still seemed at ease now, as they made their way hand-in-hand from their parking spot to the hotel. Cade hoped that meant she stopped worrying about being seen with him tonight. He couldn't wait to introduce her to his best friend, and he wasn't sure he could hide how head-over-heels he was for her when he did.

"Cade, over here!" Nate waved them down.

Cade skimmed the crowded lobby bar and smiled when

his gaze landed on his friend. He grabbed Erica's hand and led her over to their table. Half-expecting her to pull away, he breathed a silent sigh of relief when she didn't. If she was willing to hold his hand through the bar, she must not be concerned about running into her colleagues anymore. His smile widened as he approached Nate's table.

"Hey, man, glad you made it in okay!" He couldn't believe his best friend was actually here.

"Thanks for hooking us up with a room. You totally didn't have to do that." Nate stood and held out his hand.

Cade took it and wrapped his other arm around his friend, giving him a pat on the back. "I wanted to. It's not every day my best friend from college visits."

Nate stepped back and gestured to the cute redhead sitting next to him. "You've met my fiance Ashley."

"It's great to see you again." Ashley stepped out from behind the table to give Cade a hug. "Thanks for having us."

"My pleasure. It's great to see you too," Cade said, releasing her. "Nate, Ashely, this is my girlfriend, Erica."

At the word 'girlfriend,' Nate nearly spit out his drink. The look on his face was priceless. Cade couldn't suppress his chuckle as Nate opened his mouth and then closed it again. He looked like a fish out of water.

"I'm not sure what's wrong with Nate, but it's nice to meet you," Ashely said, holding out her hand to Erica and nudging Nate in the ribs with her elbow.

Nate finally found his words. "Sorry, it's just that the last time I heard you use that word was literally our freshman year of college when you were talking about your *ex*-girlfriend, Er...ica."

Cade nodded, and Nate's eyes went wide.

"Wait, you're *the* Erica?!"

Erica laughed, "I think so?"

"Yes, she's *the* Erica." Cade put his arm around her waist and pulled her into his side. He dropped a kiss on her hair before releasing her. He was so in love with this woman. It didn't matter that it had only been a few weeks. Having Erica back in his life was everything he'd always wanted. It was all he'd ever want.

They all sat, and a waiter came over to take their drink orders. Cade put his arm around Erica and felt her stiffen as she glanced around the room. With a frustrated sigh, he removed his arm from her shoulders and leaned back into his chair, hating her reaction to his touch. She was being ridiculous. He knew her job was important to her, but who from her company would be here tonight? And even if they were, Cade doubted she'd lose her promotion over dating him. She'd explain that they were high school sweethearts and that would be that.

"So, how did you two meet?" Ashley leaned in and rested her elbows on the table as though she was waiting for a good story. Cade's frustration faded as he remembered his first interaction with Erica. The story *was* pretty good.

Just before Christmas his junior year, Cade's high school guidance counselor had suggested some extracurricular activities to put on his college applications. Cade wasn't much of a joiner. He hadn't seen the point, seeing as he'd pack up and move schools again as soon as his dad finished converting the latest hotel acquisition into a Calix. Besides, the only extracurricular activity still open that semester was the dance committee.

"I'm not doing that." Cade leaned back in the chair across from the guidance counselor's desk and crossed his arms.

"I'd reconsider, if I were you. Spring sports don't start in time to include on your college applications, and with the schools you're applying to, you could definitely use the boost. It won't be that bad. Miss Evans runs a tight ship, so you'll mostly just be helping to decorate the gym."

Decorating for a dance sounded about as much fun to Cade as sticking his finger in an electrical socket, but an in with Erica Evans might just be worth it.

Cade glanced at the remarkable woman sitting next to him. Ten years later, he knew without a doubt that she was.

"You never told me that!" Erica exclaimed, making Nate and Ashley laugh. "You always said your guidance counselor *made* you join."

"He pretty much did." Cade shrugged. "Besides, it's not like I could walk in and kill my chances with you by saying, 'I'm only here because I think you're hot.'"

That made Erica laugh, too.

"I guess that wouldn't have been as smooth as offering to help me hang the mistletoe and then insisting we had to kiss," she said.

"I was just following tradition. I didn't want bad luck for the whole next year." Cade held up his hands in mock indignation. "Besides, as I recall, you weren't complaining." He grinned at Nate and Ashely. "She agreed to go out with me after that kiss."

"You guys are too cute," Ashely said, sipping her drink. It was some pink concoction, but she didn't pull a face after she tasted it, so Cade had to assume it wasn't an original created by Jason, the bar manager.

That reminded him, they only had four more days to nail everything down for New Year's Eve, and he still had to sort out the specialty drinks. He wondered what other critical tasks he'd missed lately. Jillian usually helped him manage his to-do list, and things were starting to slip without her.

"What I want to know is how you two ended up back together." Nate turned to Ashley. "Cade was the most anti-social person you've ever met the entire first semester of freshman year. He moped around our dorm room and basically refused to do anything but study. It took me months to even get him to join us at meals."

"I was not *that* bad," Cade insisted, not wanting Erica to get the wrong impression. Sure, he'd been heartbroken and didn't see the point in making friends with people who wouldn't stick around once it required them to make an effort, but he wasn't a recluse.

Nate gave him a look.

"Okay, I admit to being a little aloof at first," Cade conceded. "But I wasn't a hermit."

He glanced over at Erica. Her brow wrinkled in concern, and a small frown played across her lips. Their eyes met, and she reached over, taking his hand in hers and giving it a light squeeze. His shoulders relaxed at the small gesture, and he squeezed her hand back.

"So, how did this," Nate gestured at the two of them, "— happen?"

Cade and Erica took turns filling them in on the events of the past few weeks.

"So, what's next?" Ashely asked, looking between the two of them.

"It's only been a couple weeks." Erica laughed. "So I think what's next is meeting each other's friends and going on more dates."

"Think you'll get up to New York anytime soon?" Nate asked. "All of us miss seeing you."

Cade missed his New York friends, too.

"Not sure," he said. "There's still work to be done here, and then we'll see where the next hotel is."

"No downtime in the main office?" Nate swallowed the last of his bourbon and set the glass down on the table between them.

"Might be, I guess," Cade took a sip of his own. "Just kind of depends how quickly I get this place up and running."

Ashley glanced around at the busy lobby bar. "Seems like it's running smoothly to me."

Erica choked on the drink she just took. Coughing and sputtering, she tapped her own chest.

Cade patted her back, concerned. "You okay?"

"Yeah. Drink just went down the wrong pipe," she said, once the coughing had stopped. Cade watched her for another moment, wanting to be sure.

"Really, I'm fine now," she added, putting her hand over his on top of the table.

Now that Erica was alright, Cade allowed himself to glance around the hotel, trying to see it through a guest's eyes. He'd been so focused on the things that still needed doing that he barely noticed how far the place had come in the last few months. "I guess this place really is coming together," he mused aloud. "Once the rooftop bar is open, most of the major stuff will be done."

Erica let go of his hand and straightened in her seat. The loss of contact left his chest feeling as empty as his palm. He wondered what made her pull away. It seemed unlikely anyone she worked with had just walked in, but he guessed it wasn't impossible.

"Next time you're in town, we have to check out the new

bourbon bar in Soho. Actually, it's not too far from Lucky's," Nate said, referencing Cade's favorite pizza place.

"What I wouldn't give for some Lucky's." Cade could almost taste the New York style slices. He couldn't wait to go there with Erica one day—he knew she'd love it, too.

CHAPTER 17

Erica's heart sank as Cade and his friends continued to talk about their favorite spots in New York City. She could hear it in his voice—he missed it. In their happy getting-back-together haze, they hadn't talked about what came next, but she should've realized he wasn't planning on staying in Florida for long.

"—it's great. You'll see." Cade draped his arm around the back of her chair and massaged the back of her neck with his fingers. She used to love it when he did that, but now it made her skin prickle, like a scratchy shirt-collar.

She shrugged his hand away. "I've been to New York City, Cade. I live in Florida, not under a rock." The words came out sounding harsher than she intended.

"I know. I didn't mean to imply you hadn't traveled. It's just different living there than visiting," said Cade.

Erica stared at him, momentarily speechless. Is that what he expected? That she'd just follow him back to New York? That he'd decide on his own to go, and she'd just tag along? She had a career, too, and she was proud of it.

Her eyes pricked with tears. She stood to excuse herself before she they started to fall. Even if she wasn't sure where she and Cade stood anymore, she didn't want to make a fool of herself in front of his friends.

She took a deep breath and summoned her professional mask. "It's getting pretty late, and I have an early morning." She didn't, but they didn't have to know that. Maybe she'd get a jumpstart on her New Year's resolutions and take in an early morning spin class at the gym. "I should head home. It was great meeting you, though."

"Great meeting you, too." Ashley stood and gave Erica a quick hug.

Cade rose, too, though he didn't reach for her. The small of her back where he usually rested his hand felt empty. Was he having second thoughts about their relationship, too? The thought made her stomach turn uncomfortably.

Nate gave Erica a hug as well. "We're in town through New Year's. Maybe we can all get dinner together or something."

"If the weather holds, we could rent a boat and take you guys out on the bay," Cade said.

"Either of those sound great!" Erica pasted a smile on and hoped it lasted long enough to make her escape. It wasn't that she didn't like Nate and Ashley—they were great. She just couldn't sit by and watch as they reminded Cade of everything he was missing by being here with her. Tossing her bag over her shoulder, she turned to leave.

"Hold on, I'll walk you out," Cade said, before turning to Nate. "I'll be back in a few minutes if you guys want to hang out a little longer."

They nodded, and Erica led the way past the other bar

tables and through the lobby. She pushed her way through the revolving door, with Cade following two steps behind. They were almost to her car before Cade broke the silence.

"Are you seriously so worried about people seeing us together that you can't make it through an evening of drinks with my best friend?" Cade kept his voice low, but she could hear the frustration hiding beneath the surface.

Ironically, her stomach unknotted just a little at that. If he was mad about her PDA moratorium, then he probably wasn't having second thoughts about their relationship. But that meant she was over-reacting…again. What was it about Cade that made her constantly lose control of her emotions?

With a shaky breath, she opened her mouth to tell him he was wrong. "Cade, I—" She paused, not sure how to explain what was really bothering her.

"You know you're being ridiculous, right? You work for a one-hundred person company—if that. And of those hundred people, only a handful would recognize me. The likelihood of them being in the same place we are is so low it's negligible." He was right, but his words still stung.

Erica sighed, too tired to have this conversation now. She took a step toward him and brushed her lips against his. As always, the contact made her want more, but neither of them moved to intensify the kiss. She stepped back, eyes shining with unshed tears. "I'll see you tomorrow, Cade."

Before he could say anything else, she got in her car and drove away.

CADE'S SHOULDERS slumped as he walked back to the hotel. They'd been back together less than two weeks, and already they were coming apart at the seams. Seeing the tears *he* caused in Erica's eyes brought physical pain to his chest. He shouldn't have been so hard on her, but shoot, it stung to have her pull away from him like that. He wanted to apologize, but she drove away without giving him the chance.

CHAPTER 18

Erica stacked two coffees in one hand, balancing the top one with her chin as she pulled open the door to the hotel. The top cup wobbled as she stepped into the lobby.

She'd tossed and turned most of the previous night, hating how she left things with Cade. At least she had what she hoped would be a pleasant surprise for him this morning —she'd convinced her friend Zack, who was an excellent mixologist, to create new drink recipes for New Year's. He sent them over last night in exchange for tickets to the party for him and his new girlfriend. She hadn't realized he was dating anyone, but it sounded like he was head over heels. As soon as she had her own romance under control, she'd bug him for all the details.

Laying the penthouse keycard she got from Cade against the reader in the elevator, she pressed the button for his floor. She wasn't proud of how she'd acted the night before, but that didn't mean admitting she was wrong came easy.

She wanted to get this apology over with, so they could move on. If she was honest, she was also hoping Cade could allay her concerns about New York. It was unlikely his job would allow him to stay in Tampa forever, but she needed more time before she uprooted her whole life to follow him.

Not that she wasn't serious about Cade—she was! Heck, she'd been daydreaming about him proposing to her a few mornings ago, but they needed more than a handful of dates before they up and moved in together. And that meant Cade had to stay, at least for now. Surely he would see it that way, too.

The elevator announced its arrival to the penthouse with a ding. Erica stepped out onto the landing, hoping this conversation with Cade would go well.

She was even prepared to concede on the hiding their relationship front—at least a little. She still wanted to keep it from Harrison long enough to lock in the promotion and keep it without anyone thinking she used Cade to get there, but Cade was right that the likelihood of running into anyone who'd tell him was slim. They'd be careful until after the party, and then she'd take her chances.

She was about to knock on the door to Cade's suite, but paused when she heard Cade talking to someone on the other side.

"Are you sure? I met the guy last year, and he seemed like such a great guy. His wife and kids were so sweet, too."

"Unfortunately, being nice with a family and having a gambling addiction aren't mutually exclusive," Cade's dad said. "He took a lot of money from our Hoboken hotel."

Yikes, that sounded serious. Not wanting to eavesdrop, Erica turned to go.

"What are you going to do?" The door wasn't exactly soundproof, and Cade's voice trickled through to where she stood, waiting for the elevator to return.

"He's been fired, obviously, but he had a pretty elaborate plan involving vendor payments going, which means we're late on a lot of bills. A few of the smaller companies are refusing to work with us anymore, which means we need to find replacements or convince them otherwise.

"I need someone I trust to take over and get things back on track. It seems like you have everything running smoothly here, and I know you've been missing New York...." A rushing in Erica's ears drowned out the rest of Mr. Whitmore's words. He couldn't be sending Cade back to New York. Not yet. She just got him back.

"How soon are you thinking?" Cade's voice drew her back. She held her breath, knowing whatever Cade's dad said it would be too soon.

"We need to get this sorted out as quickly as possible. I know you'll need a week or two to sort out management here, but it seems like you've already stepped out of most of the day-to-day operations."

The elevator arrived, and Erica didn't bother to hold back her tears as she stepped inside. With each floor that she descended, her heart dropped further and further. Cade could never say 'no' to his dad. He was going to leave, and she'd be left here, trying to pick up the pieces. She should've known this would happen. She should never have let him back into her life, much less her heart.

CHAPTER 19

"I still can't believe Connelly was stealing from us." Cade stood to pace the room.

"I can't either. It's a good thing we caught it when we did. He covered his tracks pretty well, at least internally. If Ed hadn't called me about an overdue bill that was marked paid in our system, it might've gone on for far longer. Even now, it's a colossal mess to clean up." Cade's dad rubbed at his eyes. Learning one of his trusted General Managers had been stealing from him had to be a huge blow. "I know it's fast, but I was kind of hoping you could leave right after New Year's and get started next week."

Cade wished he could be the one to swoop in and fix it. He'd been looking for a way to prove to his dad he was ready to take on more of the business, and this was just the situation he'd been waiting for. But he couldn't leave now, not when things were just beginning to take shape with Erica.

"I understand why you want me there, but I can't go next week. There's still a lot to do to get this place up to Calix standards." Even as he said it, Cade knew the excuse was weak.

There was still work to do here, but he didn't need to be on site to make it happen. He just didn't want to be that far away from Erica, and they hadn't been together long enough for him to ask her to come with.

"Aren't you the one who's been trying to convince me you can oversee everything from afar?" His dad gave him a skeptical look.

Cade couldn't blame him. He'd spent the last ten months trying to convince his dad that he could oversee these openings while living in New York. Now he wished he hadn't put together such a compelling case for it.

"I have, but..." Cade trailed off, unsure of what to say next.

He wanted to tell his dad that he just got Erica back, that he couldn't risk losing her again over an unexpected move to New York, but he wasn't sure his dad would accept that response.

Cade had one other card to play, but he hated to use it. He was already struggling without Jillian. New Year's Eve was only four days away, and he still didn't have a solve for the whole drinks debacle. Jillian would've done her research and found the right person for the job, unlike Cade, who just asked the first bar manager he came across to create the speciality drinks.

Jillian was the perfect solution, though. She was already in New Jersey, and though she called Cade on Christmas to let him know her mom was out of the coma, there was still a long recovery ahead. He knew Jillian was torn between coming back to work and being there for her mom. Maybe this way, she could do both.

"What about Jillian?" The words were out of his mouth before he made a conscious decision.

"What about her? I assume she'll come with you unless you want to leave her to handle this place." His dad looked at him with raised eyebrows.

"What if Jillian took over the Hoboken hotel?" Cade said, leaning into the idea. "Her mom's out of intensive care, but still has a lot of healing to do. Jillian's really torn about coming back to work when her mom needs her in New Jersey. This could be a good solution. Plus, she's already there."

His dad looked contemplative. "It's a thought, but this is going to need someone's full attention."

"Trust me, Dad, Jillian's more detailed than I am. It's one of the reasons I love having her as my right hand. But right now, she needs to be there and I need to be here." Cade sat down on the couch, facing his dad. "It's a good solution."

His dad was quiet for a minute, and Cade hoped he wasn't gearing up to ask questions about why exactly Cade needed to stay here. Both of Cade's parents seemed genuinely happy for him and Erica at dinner last night, but Cade suspected that his dad's acceptance would diminish if he realized Cade was making business decisions based on his relationship.

"Alright, you've convinced me." His dad stood and headed for the door. "Tell Jillian to call me on Monday, and we'll come up with a game plan."

Cade sent up a silent prayer of thanks before walking him out. "Thanks, Dad. You won't regret this."

His dad stopped and put a hand on his shoulder. "I think Jillian will do a great job. I just hope you don't regret giving it to her." Then he stepped onto the waiting elevator, leaving Cade alone with his thoughts.

Cade wasn't sure what to make of his dad's parting words. It was no secret that his father thought Jillian's talents were being wasted as Cade's assistant, but he never forced Cade to give her up. He knew how much Cade depended on her. Did his dad really not think he could run this hotel alone? Cade wondered if he should be offended.

He shook his head, realizing that his dad saw right through him. A month ago, Cade would have jumped on the chance to go back to New York. Now, he couldn't imagine leaving Erica behind.

Cade smiled as he reached for the phone and dialed Jillian's number. He couldn't wait to get her onboard.

A FEW HOURS LATER, Cade sat on the too-hard couch in his suite, wondering how things went from great to bad in such a short amount of time. Jillian was thrilled with her new assignment—no surprise there. But true to his dad's warning, Cade now had some regrets about giving it to her.

He lit up his phone screen and read the set of messages between him and Erica again, trying to understand what had changed in the last twenty-four hours.

Erica:
I'm actually not feeling the best. Can we skip decorating today? I'll have a few people from my team in on Monday to help me knock it out.

Cade:

Sure, are you alright? Can I bring you anything?

The dots had appeared and reappeared before she finally responded.

Erica:

Thanks for offering, but no. I think we might have jumped in too fast here.

Cade's heart beat faster and a rushing sound filled his ears. His hands shook as he typed out a response.

Cade:

What does that mean?

Erica:

Us. This. Getting back together was a bad idea.

Cade let the phone fall from his hands.

Rereading their messages didn't make what happened any clearer. If anything, he just felt worse. Had he been too hard on her last night? Is that what this was about? He could kick himself for not just agreeing to hide their relationship for a few weeks.

After picking his phone up off the floor, he pulled up Erica's number and hit call. He half-expected her not to pick up, but she answered on the third ring.

"Hey." Her voice sounded sad, and all he wanted was to wrap his arms around her and tell her it was all going to be okay.

Cade dove right in, wanting to make sure he got this out

before she convinced herself picking up the phone was a bad idea, too. "I'm sorry about last night. I get how important this promotion is to you, and if you need us to keep our relationship quiet for a few more weeks, I can live with that."

Erica sighed. "It's not about that, Cade. Our relationship ended without closure last time, and neither of us really let it go. But you were always meant to go to New York. It's home for you. We're not the same people we were ten years ago. We grew up, Cade, and we want different things out of life. I'm never going to be one of those arm-candy women you like to date."

Something cracked inside his chest. He couldn't believe what he was hearing. "The only thing I want is you!"

It was true. He'd give up everything to keep her in his life, because none of it mattered without her. How could she not see that?

"I love you, Er," he whispered.

"I love you, too, Cade." Erica's voice cracked. "A part of me will always love you. But one day we'll both wake up resenting the sacrifices we had to make to keep this relationship going, and I don't want that for us."

"You can't mean that," said Cade, grasping for anything that would keep her from leaving him.

"I'm sorry Cade. I really wanted this to work, too." The phone went silent for a moment, before she added, "Don't worry about New Year's. Everything's set. My team will be out to help with decorations and setup on Monday, and I'll still oversee the event itself. I have at least as much riding on this as you do, so I'm planning on seeing it through."

The bar opening hadn't even crossed his mind. His whole heart was on the line here, and somehow she was talking about work. "Erica—", he began.

"I have to go, Cade."

His heart splintered even more. He wasn't sure he'd survive losing her again, but it was pretty clear that he didn't have a choice.

The real kick in the teeth of it all was that he made his choice already—he chose *her*. Which meant now he was on his own. He couldn't walk that back, either. Even if he was willing to tell his dad he changed his mind, he couldn't un-promote Jillian.

CHAPTER 20

Erica sat cross-legged on her soft leather couch, laptop open on her lap, the T.V. on in the background. She swiped a tear off her cheek and reached for another tissue. She tried to shove aside her feelings and focus on work, but the screen kept blurring. Stupid tears.

Until he called, she'd been fine. Why couldn't he just leave it alone?

Another sob found its way up her throat. Ending their relationship now was supposed to make things easier, but it didn't. She felt empty inside, her broken heart held together by tape and glue. But an unhappy ending was inevitable for her and Cade, and as much as this hurt, it was better to admit that now, before they got in even deeper. Before there was nothing left of her heart to piece together. Before it ruined her career.

Getting involved with a client was stupid, especially with a promotion at stake. It was like she told Cade. They got caught up in old feelings—except right now, those feelings seemed devastatingly current.

She let out a shuddering breath and set the laptop on the coffee table before curling into a fetal position on the couch. With a soft throw tucked tightly around her, she closed her eyes and listened as the happy couple on television promised nothing would ever come between them again. If only love was as easy as they made it seem in the movies.

She must have drifted off, because the next time she opened her eyes, it was dark out and a different couple filled the screen. She turned off the TV, not wanting to watch another love story play out on screen with her own heart this raw. Promising herself she'd feel better in the morning, she peeled herself off the couch and got ready for bed.

THE NEXT MORNING, sunlight filtered through Erica's curtains, lighting up her bedroom with its rays. That, with the cheerful sound of birds singing outside, was a direct contrast to how she felt. She pulled the comforter over her head so it filtered out most of the light and noise. Taking a deep breath, she blinked back a fresh batch of tears.

No. No way.

She wasn't doing this.

She wouldn't spend another day wallowing.

It was one thing to indulge herself yesterday afternoon. It was quite another to spend the entire weekend in bed. She flung the comforter off and sat up. Ending things with Cade was the right thing to do. She'd spent most of her adult life wondering what might have been with him. And now she knew—it wouldn't have worked out, anyway.

She put herself through the motions of getting ready, even though she didn't have anywhere to be. Maybe she'd see what her friends were up to. She'd barely seen any of them since she started working on the New Year's party.

Wrapped in a towel after her shower, she frowned at her reflection in the mirror. Her eyes were puffy and raw from crying. Maybe she wouldn't be going out today. No amount of makeup would hide *that,* and she wanted to distract herself from Cade, not talk about him.

Alright, new plan. She'd get caught up on all the non-Calix work that had been piling up.

Dressed in real clothes—jeans and a t-shirt—she made coffee, adding a little too much peppermint mocha creamer to the mug before carrying it to the living room. Careful not to spill her coffee, she found a comfortable position on the couch. After flipping through the channels three times, she settled on a reality show for noise, then fired up her laptop.

It took her a full hour to clear her inbox. Just another thing Cade messed up for her. The thought of him brought another wave of sadness. Determined not to let him distract her any further, she opened the project plan for her first January event. Cringing at the number of red due dates, she lost herself in vendor contracts and follow-ups. A notification popped up on her screen and she clicked over to her messages.

Zack:
Did Cade like the new and improved cocktails?

Her heart clenched at seeing his name on her screen. *No, I've been too busy breaking up with him to share the recipes.* She didn't want to say that to Zack, though.

Erica:

We haven't had a chance to try them yet, but I'm sure they'll be great. Your drinks always are.

Zack:

Haha, thanks.

Zack:

Looking forward to meeting Cade on New Year's. And I can't wait to introduce you to Holly. I've only known her a short time, but I already can't imagine life without her. I think she's the one. Is that insane?

Erica didn't think it was insane. That's how she felt about Cade when they first started dating, and she was pretty sure she wasn't crazy. That didn't mean she hadn't been wrong, though. A tear slid down her cheek.

Erica:

*No, it's not insane. I'm happy for you. Now I'm really excited to meet her. *grinning face emoji**

Another tear slipped past her defenses as she hit send. She was genuinely happy for her friend, but the smiling yellow face was a lie.

She found Zack's email with the drink recipes and forwarded it to Cade, adding a brief message that sounded even more formal than her work emails usually did. The screen was blurry by the time she finished.

She sniffed and reached for a tissue. If just typing his name into an email turned her into a sobbing mess, what was she going to do when she had to see him face-to-face? She couldn't just not show up. Tomorrow was the last day of preparation, the next day was New Year's Eve, and her entire career depended on this event going well.

CHAPTER 21

Cade sat at one of three tables next to the espresso bar in the Calix lobby, drinking a coffee. He shouldn't be around people, especially hotel employees, in his current emotional state, but he could only spend so much time in his suite before the walls started closing in. He watched a twenty-something couple stroll through the lobby, hand-in-hand. The man whispered something in her ear. Cade's throat tightened painfully as they both laughed. Just two days ago, that had been him and Erica.

"Missed you last night." Nate's cheerful voice broke into his thoughts. "Did you get that work thing figured out?"

"Mostly." There was no work thing. He just didn't feel like being social after being dumped. "Did you and Ashley have a nice dinner?" He changed the subject, hoping Nate wouldn't ask for details.

"Yeah, it was great. Thanks for the restaurant recommendation."

"No problem. Glad it was good." Cade tried to inject a bit

of enthusiasm into his voice as he turned to look at his friend.

Based on his athletic attire and slightly messy hair, Nate was on his way back from the gym. That was a good idea, actually. Maybe a workout would do Cade some good.

"Everything okay?" Nate took the chair next to him, a concerned look on his face.

No. "I'm just stressed about this New Year's bar opening, and it sucks not having my assistant here to help."

And Erica broke up with me. Cade wasn't sure why he didn't just come out and say it. It wasn't like Nate wouldn't figure it out, but he wasn't ready to talk about it yet. Talking about it made it real, and Cade desperately didn't want it to be real. Erica was the one. She'd always been the one. She was *it* for him—only she didn't feel the same way, and he had no clue what to do with that.

"Sounds like a day out on the water is just what you need, then." Nate gave him a light punch on the shoulder. "When's Erica getting here?"

"She's not." Cade sighed and rubbed a hand over his face. "I'm not sure I can go anymore, either. I have too much to do around here."

"Wait, rewind. Why is Erica not coming? I thought you said the boat rental was her idea."

"Because she decided getting back together was a mistake." Cade nearly choked on the words. He'd been right. Saying them out loud made it worse.

"Whoa. I wasn't expecting that." Nate shook his head.

"That makes two of us, because I wasn't, either." Cade picked at the corner of the cardboard sleeve on his coffee. "Anyway, you and Ashley should go enjoy the boat. I'm going to pass."

"No way. That's not happening."

"What do you mean?"

"I'm not letting you push me away. What exactly happened, anyway? It seemed like Erica was a little upset when she left the other night, but you seemed good when you came back from walking her out."

"I guess she decided otherwise. She said we want different things. But that's impossible for her to know, since we never even talked about it." Cade's voice cracked a little. "Sure, I was kind of hard on her about wanting to keep our relationship a secret from her coworkers, but that's temporary."

"From where I sit, it looks like both of you are falling into old habits. She sees conflict and runs. You pull away from everyone who cares about you. Except I'm not letting you get away with it this time. You're my best friend and I never get to see you. You're going to come out today and have a good time with Ash and me."

"Not sure I'm capable of having a good time right now. I feel like I can barely breathe. This is the first time I've been out of my room since she told me we were over."

A notification popped up on his phone, and his heart quickened at seeing Erica's name on the screen.

"It's Erica," he told Nate.

"I'll order coffee while you get that. Maybe she realized she made a mistake." Nate stood and walked to the counter.

Cade barely registered his friend walking away, feeling hopeful for the first time since yesterday. Maybe Nate was right and Erica changed her mind. They were meant for each other—she'd just needed time to see it, too.

Then he saw the Erica notification was an email, not a

text. Disappointment rose like bile in the back of his throat as he read the message sharing the drink recipes her friend fixed for New Year's. He swallowed hard. Of course, it was about the stupid party.

He shook his head and clenched his jaw against the tears he could feel pricking at the back of his eyes. *At least the drinks thing is solved,* he thought sarcastically. For all he cared, they could serve the crappy ones—it would serve Erica right if she had to deal with all the complaints. Might even jeopardize her promotion.

He sighed, knowing he could never do that to her. What was wrong with him, that even as she tore his heart to shreds, he wanted her to succeed? He wanted her to be happy—he just wished she could be happy *with him.*

Frowning, he forwarded the email to the bar manager and asked him to make sure the bartenders working the event knew how to make the drinks.

"You alright there?" Nate came back to Cade's table carrying two coffees.

"No." Cade clenched his jaw harder, refusing to let his emotions get the better of him.

"You're coming out with us today, whether you like it or not. You can wallow on the boat in the sun." Nate stood and gave Cade's shoulder a squeeze. "We'll meet you back down here in an hour and a half."

Nate picked up his coffee and walked away before Cade could respond. He only made it a few steps before he stopped and turned around.

For a second, Cade wondered if his friend had changed his mind and was giving him a free pass for the day.

Instead, Nate gave him some tough love. "Listen, instead

of feeling sorry for yourself, maybe you should come up with a plan to get her back. It's obvious the two of you have something special. If you love her, fight for her. Don't just let her walk away."

The next afternoon, Cade sat at an empty table in the rooftop bar, sneaking glances at the elevator. Despite Pauline's insistence that Erica was sick, he was convinced she'd decide to show up. It had to be killing her not to be here with her team the day before the event. He watched as his hotel staff hauled in glassware, and Erica's team put the finishing touches on the decor.

He'd tried to pitch in and help when he first arrived, but both Pauline and Will said he was just getting in the way. He told himself he stayed to 'supervise,' but really, he was just waiting for Erica.

With a sigh, he leaned back in his seat. He should just leave and find Nate or his parents. Both would welcome the chance to spend more time with him. Instead, here he sat.

He swallowed the ball of disappointment that crept up his throat when he realized Erica's team was just about finished. Even without her, they'd done a great job. The party was on track, but his plan to win her back had already hit a major snag. She wasn't going to show.

He came back from boating yesterday in better spirits than he thought possible. After listening to him spill his guts, Nate and Ashely had convinced him that he needed to talk to Erica in person. He owed her an apology for dismissing her concerns about their relationship's impact on her job. He'd offer to keep things low key for as long as she wanted. Anything was better than not having her at all.

If she'd hear him out for that long—and Ashley insisted she would—he'd insist they have an actual conversation about what they wanted for the future. His answer was easy. He wanted to be with her, and he'd do whatever it took to make that happen. If she wanted to stay here permanently, great. Cade's dad had agreed to let him handle the next hotel opening from New York, and there was no reason he couldn't run it from here instead.

By the time they returned the boat, he'd been convinced it would all work out. Now, as he waited for her to arrive, his good mood was slipping away. He picked up a piece of the black and gold confetti that decorated the table. He'd been positive she wouldn't be able to stay away today. Not when her event started in twenty-eight hours. Flicking the confetti away, he admitted to himself that he'd been wrong.

Maybe she really *was* sick.

He wondered if missing today would affect her promotion. It shouldn't, since everything got done, but what did he know? It had taken a lecture from Ashely on double standards in the workplace for him to grasp how serious dating a client could be for Erica. He hated how much of a jerk he'd been about it in the parking lot a few nights ago.

Thinking back on the reason for that fight, he realized it might be a good thing that this afternoon didn't go as planned. Erica was already under enough pressure to pull this party off. The last thing she needed was the added stress of hiding their relationship. As much as he wanted her back right away, their relationship could wait another few days.

In the meantime, though, he had an idea to show how much he cared about her and her career.

He pulled out his phone and dashed off an email to Harrison. Surely a glowing review from a client—one she definitely wasn't dating—would push things in the right direction.

CHAPTER 23

Harrison's name flashed across Erica's phone screen. Tugging the crocheted blanket more tightly around her shoulders, she steeled herself to answer it.

She had no idea why he'd be calling today. Was he going to call her out on staying home sick while her team did all the setup?

No, that was just her guilt talking.

Harrison didn't know she wasn't sick. She slid her finger across the screen to answer, then put it on speaker.

"This is Erica," she said automatically.

"Hey, it's Harrison. How are you feeling? I heard you were under the weather."

"Still a little stuffed up, but a lot better than over the weekend." Erica didn't actually feel better about breaking up with Cade, but it was true that her tears slowed down enough for her sinuses to clear.

"Glad to hear you're improving. Anyway, I'm calling because I got an email from Cade Whitmore today."

Erica clung to her throw blanket like a lifeline. An over-whelming sense of dread flooded through her body, drenching her in a cold sweat. Cade wasn't exactly happy with her the last time they spoke. What if he called her out for not showing up today? Or, even worse, what if Cade called the whole event off so he didn't have to see her again?

"He said he's really impressed with how you handled their event. He also mentioned that you took care of a couple of things that should've been the hotel's responsibility. Sounds like you really went above and beyond," said Harrison.

Erica pressed her lips together as his words sunk in. A ball of warmth expanded through her chest as she realized what they meant. Cade knew how much this promotion meant to her. He must have guessed she was freaking out about not being there today. Despite the way she ended things with him, Cade went to bat for her.

"That's great!" she finally managed, her eyes glistening with unshed tears.

"Congratulations, Erica. I know I had my doubts, but it looks like you did it. As long as tomorrow night goes well, you'll be the new Director of Events."

A slow smile spread across Erica's face. "Thanks, Harrison."

"Are you feeling well enough to work the party tomor-row? If not, I can step in."

"I'll be there. I should be back to normal by then." That was a lie. She didn't even know what normal was anymore, but there was no way she was missing this event.

~

ERICA DOUBLE-CHECKED that the mascara in her hand was waterproof before swiping it over her eyelashes. She'd managed to keep her emotions in check so far today, but seeing Cade tonight would bring them all back to the surface. She had to face him, though. The promotion was almost hers, but the event still had to be flawless, and she needed to be there to make sure everything went as planned.

She was sliding into her dress when an incoming video call from Julia lit up her phone. She pulled up her zipper and reached for her phone, answering just before the call timed out. "Hey, Julia!"

"Erica! I'm engaged!" Julia's smile lit up her entire face as she held her left hand up to the camera so Erica could see the ring. It was perfect for Julia.

"Congratulations! It's beautiful! I'm so happy for you!" Erica's voice came out a little too high.

She was excited for her cousin, but the news of Julia's engagement just reminded Erica of what she didn't have herself. Knowing she couldn't spoil Julia's night with her own news, she pasted a smile on her face and asked when and how Brad popped the question.

She propped the phone up on her dresser, and threaded a pair of earrings through her ears while listening to her cousin's engagement story.

"Did you know he was planning to ask you today?" Erica asked, digging through her jewelry box for a necklace.

"After you put the idea of a New Year's proposal in my head, I thought he might do it tonight. I definitely didn't expect him to get down on one knee and pull out a ring in the middle of our hike, though." Julia's giddy excitement was obvious, even through the small screen.

Still rooting through her jewelry box, Erica's fingers landed on the little gold bow from Cade. A twisting pain blossomed in her chest at the sight of it. It'd be perfect for her dress tonight, but there was no way she could wear it. She bit her lip as she laid it back inside the box, trying to keep the emotion off her face. She had no intention of putting a damper on Julia's big news by talking about her own breakup.

"Erica?"

"Sorry, I'm listening," Erica said, selecting a different necklace and fastening it around her neck.

"I asked if you were excited about tonight," Julia said. "It's your first New Year's back with Cade."

"More nervous than anything. I'll be working an event that my entire career depends on." That was true, but her answer was still a big fat lie by omission.

"If I know you, you have a plan and a back-up plan for everything. I'm sure it'll be great," said Julia.

"If only I had a back-up plan for being around Cade tonight," Erica mumbled under her breath, taking one last glance at her reflection in the mirror before opening her closet to find a purse and shoes.

"Wait, what?"

"Nothing." Erica searched her closet for the shoes that went with her dress.

"Oh, no. I heard what you said. What happened with Cade?" Darn Julia and her freaky-good hearing.

Erica sighed, knowing her cousin wouldn't let this drop. "It didn't work out. Look, I don't want to be a wet blanket on your engagement day. I'll call you later this week and give you the scoop, okay?"

"No, not okay, because you've been in love with Cade Whitmore since you were seventeen. I can't imagine that whatever happened is bad enough to throw that away."

"He's going back to New York."

"So?" Julia blinked at her through the screen.

"So, he's leaving me again." Erica sat down on her bed, blinking back tears. She would *not* ruin her makeup before she even left.

"I don't get it. Why would he start dating you again if he's leaving, and isn't open to a long distance relationship?"

"He didn't know. He was planning on staying longer, but something came up, and his dad wants him in New York." Erica twirled a piece of hair around her finger. A sinking feeling spread through her stomach as the conversation she and Cade had on the beach echoed through her mind. The one where she'd asked him if he thought long distance would've worked.

"You're the one who refused to try," He'd said.

Was she doing the same thing again?

She reached down to pull on her left shoe.

"Even if he was open to being long distance, it's too soon for that." She said, trying to convince herself as much as her cousin. "It's only been two weeks. That's way too short a time to decide you're not just exclusive, but doing it from eleven hundred miles apart."

"Except it's not a stranger you just met. It's Cade!" Julia said, sounding exasperated.

Erica hated that she was right. She glanced at the clock as she pulled on her other shoe. She needed to leave now if she wanted to arrive before guests started pouring in.

"Sorry, Julia. I've got to go or I'm going to be late. I'll call you tomorrow, though, okay? Congratulations again to you and Brad." Her voice was too high again. "I can't wait to help you plan the wedding!"

CHAPTER 24

By the time she stepped into the hotel elevator, Erica's stomach was in knots. The party tonight would make or break her career, but that wasn't what had her insides feeling twisty. She'd been second guessing her decision to end things with Cade all the way here.

The doors opened, and she stepped out. Her heart gave a little stutter when she spotted Cade across the room. She admired the way he filled out his perfectly tailored suit as he talked to Will and another hotel employee she hadn't met. He was everything she'd ever wanted in a partner. Kind, thoughtful, smart, and handsome, Cade was the whole package. She'd never find anyone else as right for her as he was.

She swallowed hard, trying to soothe the ache in her throat at the thought of losing him forever. Julia was right. She didn't break up with Cade because they had irreconcilable visions for the future. She cut and ran because she was afraid of being hurt. Only now, she was even more afraid of spending the rest of her life without him.

Suddenly, she was no longer second-guessing. Cade's

relocation didn't have to mean they were over. She was still in love with him, and ending their relationship had been a huge mistake.

She took several purposeful strides toward him before remembering where they were and what she was here for. She hated the idea of going one more minute without talking to Cade, but she had to stay professional tonight if she wanted to return from the holidays with a new job title. Hurling herself into Cade's arms and begging him to give them another chance was about as far from professional as she could get.

A part of her wanted to do it, anyway. There were plenty of event planner jobs in New York City—except that almost all of them would be easier to get if she already had this promotion on her resume. She couldn't let her feelings interfere with her job. Drawing in a deep breath, she turned away from Cade. The only way to get through tonight was to avoid him altogether.

She just hoped tomorrow wasn't too late. What if Cade left before they could talk? What if it was already too late? She hadn't heard from him since the breakup—not even a thank you for the drink recipes. Sure, he'd emailed Harrison yesterday, but he hadn't even copied her on it. Maybe he was done with her, and that email was his way of saying goodbye. Her eyes prickled with tears at the thought. Blinking them back, she headed for the DJ booth to make sure he knew how they wanted the countdown to go.

Her eyes kept finding Cade as she made a circuit of the restaurant. She forced herself to smile as she said 'hello' to all the employees and vendors who were helping them bring the event to life. If Cade decided it was over, there was nothing she could do about it tonight. And if he left for New York tomorrow, she'd get on a plane to talk to him there. All she could do was hope he'd give her another chance when they spoke.

As the first guests trickled in, a sense of pride flowed through her. Her team had done an amazing job with the space, and judging by the approving murmurs she heard from the guests, the evening was off to a great start.

THE BEGINNING of the night went by in a blur. Erica almost started to relax as she sipped on a glass of champagne—one of two drinks she'd allow herself for the night. People seemed to be enjoying themselves. The place was full, but the bar lines weren't overly long. The sandwiches were on the buffet line now, but the passed hors d'oeuvres had been a hit.

Even Harrison and his wife looked like they were having a good time, dancing to a slow song on the dance floor. It wasn't midnight yet, but all signs pointed to the event being a success. She'd even managed to avoid being near Cade so far, though she wasn't sure how—unless he was avoiding her, too. She couldn't decide whether to be disappointed or grateful, if he was.

"T-minus two hours until midnight," the DJ called out, switching the music to something a little faster. Erica watched as several couples, including Harrison, exited the dance floor. Another set of dancers, who appreciated the faster song, soon took their place.

Erica felt someone step up beside her. She knew it was Cade without needing to turn and look. It had always been like that with them. Every nerve in her body seemed to light up whenever he was near.

"Great party," he whispered in her ear, his lips so close she could feel his breath on her skin.

She inhaled softly, breathing in his citrus and bergamot scent. A shiver raced down her spine, her traitorous body siding with her heart instead of her head. She stood paralyzed, unsure how to handle to having him so close. Her first inclination was to run—being near him was making her *feel* things, and she couldn't let her emotions take over tonight. Did he know what effect he was having on her?

His breath on her ear had always been her kryptonite. The electric pull she'd always felt with him was almost too much to resist as she turned to look at him.

"I know you're working," he said, his lips almost brushing her ear. "But I just wanted to say thank you. This is amazing. Even my dad's impressed. He hasn't come up with one 'next time I would do this differently' all night." Cade's huff tickled the skin on her neck. "I could never have pulled this off without you. So thanks."

The corners of her mouth quirked up. "We always did make a good team." She paused. There was so much more she wanted to say to him, but this was not the time. "Sorry for being MIA the last few days."

He raised an eyebrow and looked at her like she might be out of her mind. She guessed it was a weird thing to say, given the circumstances.

"Cade, can we talk?" The words were out of her mouth before she had time to think them through, but she wasn't willing to take them back. Her heart pounded as she waited for his reply. It didn't matter that they were in the middle of the New Year's party. She couldn't wait another minute to tell him how she felt.

"Now?" His eyes searched hers, like he was trying to

figure out what she couldn't wait until tomorrow to discuss. She thought she saw a glimmer of hope in them, too, but it could just be a trick of the light.

"If that's okay?" She held her breath, wanting him to say yes, but terrified about what it would mean for her career if he did.

"Yeah, sure." Cade started to reach for her hand, but pulled back abruptly. Frowning, he shoved his hand in his pants pocket instead. "There's a quiet hallway behind the kitchen."

She let out her breath and followed him through the crowded bar to the empty service hallway. Her heart was in her throat by the time he turned to face her.

"Cade, I…" Erica started, struggling to put her feelings into words. "I made a mistake."

Cade leaned a shoulder against the wall, looking contemplative.

"I'm still in love with you," she continued, hope blooming in her chest as Cade's lips quirked up in a smile. "I'll always be in love with you. I don't want this to be over. I don't want *us* to be over. I want to figure things out."

Cade was quiet for a moment before whispering, "I want that, too." He cleared his throat. "And I'm sorry, too," he said in a normal tone. "I should have been more understanding about you wanting to keep our relationship quiet until after your promotion. I didn't really get how much it could impact your job until Ashley set me straight."

"I've missed you so much these last few days," Erica said. "I know that's stupid, but—"

Cade pressed a finger against her lips. "It's not stupid. I've missed you, too. I can't stand the thought of losing you, Erica. Not when I just got you back."

Tears sprung to her eyes as he wrapped her in a hug and dropped a kiss on top of her head. She never wanted to leave his embrace, not when being in his arms felt so right. "I know we'll have to be long distance for a while, but I'm willing to make that work if you are."

Cade stepped back and gave her an odd look. "What do you mean, we'll have to be long distance?"

CHAPTER 25

It felt like he was on one of those theme park rides that stops suddenly, and then launches backward. Erica still wanted him, and knowing that made him want to shout with joy. But he had no idea what she meant by the long distance thing.

"Why would we have to be long distance?" His heart thumped faster in his chest. He certainly didn't have plans to go anywhere, but maybe she did. Was her promotion taking her out of central Florida?

Her brows knit together. "You're head back to New York soon."

"No." Cade shook his head. "I'm not. My dad wanted me to, but I gave the job to Jillian so I could stay here with you."

Erica's eyes widened and a guilty look crossed her face.

"Wait, how did you even know about that?" It wasn't like they'd discussed it—Erica had broken up with him before he had a chance to tell her.

"I came by early on Saturday. I was about to knock on your door when I heard your dad mention something about an employee embezzling." She reached for her necklace and began fiddling with the pendant on the end. It wasn't the bow he gave her, which bothered him more that it should have.

"I swear I didn't mean to eavesdrop." Her words spilled out faster. "I pressed the button to call the elevator back as fast as I could, but your door isn't super soundproof and your dad said he needed you in New York right away, and you'd just been talking about how much you missed it with Nate and Ashley, and—"

"And you assumed I'd go." Cade's jaw clenched, but it wasn't really anger that had his back teeth grinding together. It was pain, gut-wrenching pain. The woman he loved didn't trust him. She was the center of his universe—he'd do anything for her. Meanwhile, she thought so little of him she didn't bother to ask what his plans were, just presumed the worst and ended things. Maybe he was the one who made the mistake. Trusting her with his heart again was a one-way ticket to misery.

"Maybe you were right, Erica. We do want different things. I didn't have to think twice about giving up New York—or my assistant—to be with you. Heck, I probably gave up my dad's approval, because goodness knows, I'm won't be able to do my job half as well without Jillian. And you... you just cut and ran the minute things got hard. You didn't even *talk* to me first. You just *assumed.* And then you walked away."

"Cade, I'm here now." Erica's eyes glistened with tears. Usually that would be enough to stop him in his tracks, but right now, he was too upset to care.

"And how long is that going to last? Huh? Until I actually have to move again for work? Until someone questions your promotion? Until Calix wants to hire your agency for another event?"

"Cade, that's not fair," Erica whispered, blinking back tears. A single tear escaped and tracked down her face.

"You want to talk about fair? If you told me you wanted to move to Timbuktu, I'd find a way to come with you. You didn't even give me a chance to tell you about New York before breaking up with me."

"That was a mistake. I said I was sorry." Erica swiped at the tear running down her face.

Cade felt a twinge of guilt. He hated to see her upset. But relationships were a two-way street, and right now, he didn't trust her not to drive in the opposite direction as soon as something didn't go as planned. Being in a relationship meant compromise, but he couldn't be the only one to give. He couldn't be with someone who never put him first.

He opened his mouth to tell her that, but closed it again before the words could escape. Rubbing a hand over his face, he closed his eyes and let out a deep exhale. This wasn't the place, or the time. They had an event to run.

"Let's just not do this right now. We have a party to get back to." He turned and walked back toward the steady beat of the music. With each step, the air around him seemed harder to breathe.

He glanced back once before pressing through the door to the party. Erica still stood in the same spot, her jaw slack, as though she couldn't quite believe what had just happened. Well, make that two of them, because he never thought in a million years he'd be the one to walk away from her.

Music and the low rumble of voices washed over him as he made his way through the restaurant, heading for the door that led outside. The room was too hot, and he needed fresh air. The night air was cool, so the retractable windows were up. Through them, he could see only a handful of guests lingering on the rooftop patio. They needed to get space heaters, so the entire space could be used no matter the temperature. He put that on his mental to-do list—a list he'd have plenty of time to accomplish now that he was stuck here, alone.

"Cade, wait!" Erica's voice carried over the music. He turned to see her striding purposefully toward him. A few people, including her boss, stopped their conversations to watch. Cade wondered if she knew she was causing a bit of a scene.

"People are staring," he said when she reached him.

"Let them." She reached her arms up and clasped her hands behind his neck. "I choose you, Cade." Warmth radiated through his chest at her words. He'd waited a decade to hear her say them. "You're what matters. I don't care where we live, and I'd rather lose my promotion than lose you."

She pressed her lips to his, sending sparks of electricity down his spine. Wrapping his arms around her, he parted his lips and swept his tongue against hers. She pulled him closer, deepening the kiss, choosing him with her actions and her words.

They were both a little breathless when they finally broke apart.

"I choose you, too." He whispered.

The rest of the room faded away as he leaned down to kiss her again.

～

Every nerve in Erica's body stood at attention as Cade leaned in for another kiss. His lips grazed hers, softly at first, before becoming more insistent. She matched his intensity with her own, wanting everything he had to give.

"One hour until midnight!" The DJ's voice broke through her blissful haze.

She jerked a back with a flash of panic. She'd just kissed Cade in front of everyone, including her boss. It only took one look at Cade's smile to dispel that feeling, though. She might lose out on the promotion, but she had him, and that was all that mattered.

She pressed up on her tiptoes and brushed her lips softly against his. "I love you, Cade."

"I love you, too," he whispered as the DJ switched over to a slow song.

Cade took Erica's hand, leading her onto the dance floor. She laced her fingers behind his neck, enjoying the feeling of his hands at her waist as they swayed to the music.

"That was some kiss." Zack danced up next to them, his arms around a pretty brunette.

Erica fought a blush. "Hey, Zack. This is my boyfriend, Cade." A warm glow spread through her whole body as she glanced up against Cade. He was hers, and she'd never let him go again.

Zack cleared his throat.

"Sorry," Erica couldn't stop her blush this time. "Cade, this is Zack. He's the one who saved our butts with the New Year's drinks."

"Nice to meet you, Zack. I was hoping Erica would connect us. Based on the compliments we're getting on tonight's specials, I'd love to have your help with the regular drink menu."

"Sure," Zack said, looking a little embarrassed at the attention. "Erica, Cade, this is my girlfriend, Holly."

"It's great to meet you!" Holly held out her hand.

"Great to meet you, too!" Erica said, shaking it. "You're lucky. Zack's one of the good ones."

"I'm the lucky one." Holly looked at Zack with pure adoration. Erica recognized that look—it was the same one she wore herself when she looked at Cade. Her heart swelled with happiness for her friend.

As Zack and Holly danced off, she noticed Harrison standing near the bar, glaring her way. A flurry of butterflies started up in her stomach, threatening to overtake her happiness. She made her choice, and now she had to live with the consequences. She might as well go face the music now.

"I'm going to go check in with Harrison." Erica gave Cade's hand a squeeze as she stepped away.

"Good luck," he said, tugging her back to plant a quick kiss on her forehead. "And hurry back. I have a surprise for you at midnight."

"A kiss?" Erica guessed.

"I'm not sure a kiss is much of a surprise, but that too." Cade's eyes twinkled.

Erica looked at the large digital clock next to the DJ booth. She had almost twenty minutes to wait. It was tempting to stay and badger Cade into telling her what the surprise was, but she should deal with Harrison first.

Squaring her shoulders, she weaved through the crowd toward her boss, trying to gauge how mad he was. The lump in her throat grew as she walked. It wasn't just the promotion she was worried about. She could lose her job over this. Technically, there wasn't a policy against kissing clients in the middle of events, though she suspected her actions tonight might be the start of one.

Harrison's gaze seemed less threatening the closer she got. Wait, was he smiling?

"Harrison. Hey," Erica said, trying to sound normal, even though her heart was threatening to beat its way out of her rib cage.

"Congratulations, Erica. The turnout for this party has been amazing. I overheard the guy at the door saying they even filled up the lobby bar with people trying to get last-minute tickets after they sold out. Everyone I've talked to has said what a great time they're having. You really pulled this off."

Erica blinked, unable to believe her ears. Was he congratulating her on a job well done? Had he not seen the kiss with Cade?

"Don't look so surprised. What happened to that confidence you had a month ago when you strolled into my office asking for Madeline's job?" Harrison sipped his drink—Zack's 'Out with the Old-Fashioned,' if she wasn't mistaken.

"Um, I, well…" Erica shrugged and gestured to Cade.

Understanding filled Harrison's eyes. "You thought I might not approve of your extra-curricular activities."

Erica nodded, unable to speak around the lump in her throat.

"I can't say I've changed my stance on hooking up with clients. It's not something I encourage." Harrison's words made Erica grimace. "But in your case, I'm happy to make an exception. You told me from day one that you and Cade had history. It would be foolish of me to punish one of my best employees over finding her way back to a man who's obviously crazy about her." Harrison's serious face morphed into a grin. "Now, go enjoy the party. You can worry about moving into your new office after the holiday."

"You mean I got it?" Erica squealed, pinching herself to see if she was dreaming.

"You got it," Harrison laughed as she launched herself at him, enveloping him in a grateful hug.

"Thanks, Harrison."

"Don't thank me, you earned it. Although now that I think about it, you might want to thank Pauline. She's been lobbying pretty hard for you." Harrison took a glass of champagne from a passing waiter, handing it to his wife as he waved Erica off.

"Ten minutes until midnight!" The DJ announced as Erica made her way back to Cade.

"C'mon." Cade grabbed her hand and led her toward the door to the terrace.

"Outside?" She paused. It was a cool night, and she didn't have a sweater.

"It'll give you the best view," he promised, wrapping her arm around her.

The gesture filled her with enough warmth to brave the cooler temperature outside. She stepped through the door and let him lead her to the railing. She shivered a little, unsure whether she was reacting to the breeze or Cade's presence beside her.

"Here, take my jacket," he offered, pulling it off and draping it around her shoulders. She gave a subtle sniff, enjoying the smell of citrus and bergamot that now enveloped both of them.

"Five. Four. Three. Two." The countdown began inside.

Cade pressed his lips to hers as the first firework exploded in front of them.

They broke apart to watch as another, and another, and another lit up the sky.

"Cade, did you do this?"

He gave a casual shrug, but the look on his face told her how excited he was to have pulled this off. "My girl wanted fireworks."

Sparks ran along her skin where his hand grazed her hand. Little did he know, it only took a touch to light up her world.

EPILOGUE

The three-carat diamond was heavy in Cade's pocket as he walked through Central Park with Erica.

Moving to New York had been her idea. Without him saying a word, she found a handful of major clients in the city and convinced Harrison to let her start an office there. It was just Erica for now, but he knew she'd grow it into something great.

She shivered as a cold gust of wind swept down the pathway.

He wrapped his arm around her shoulders, pulling her close as he checked his watch again. Everything about tonight was planned out perfectly. The carriage, complete with blankets and hot cocoa, would take them for a ride around the park. After he proposed, it would drop them off at a nearby restaurant, where friends and family waited to congratulate them on their engagement—and ring in the new year.

Except the carriage was three minutes late.

"Remind me why we're walking so slowly through the park tonight?" Erica snuggled deeper into his side. "I'm a Florida girl and it's freezing!"

As though to prove her point, a dusting of snow began to accumulate on the ground around them.

"I thought you loved the park," he said, noting that the horse and carriage were now five minutes late. As subtly as possible, he slipped his phone from his pocket, his fingers brushing the ring box.

He glanced at the screen. No messages. The carriage should be here by now. Erica or Jillian would've had a back-up plan, but Cade arranged this all himself—and it didn't occur to him that he might need one.

The clatter of hooves on pavement got louder as the carriage approached. Relief flooded through him as Erica turned to look toward the noise. She watched in wonder as the horse came to a stop in front of her.

"Sorry I'm late," said the driver. "I went back to grab an extra blanket. It's cold out tonight!"

"This is for us?" Erica covered her mouth with her mitten-clad hands. "I've always wanted to ride in one of these!"

"I know. You mention it every time we see one." Cade laughed. That was how he came up with the idea.

Taking her hand, he helped her up the portable stairs the driver set next to the carriage, then climbed in next to her. He tucked the blanket around the front of their shoulders, and she settled in with a sigh.

Cade pulled her closer as the carriage started up, enjoying her warmth for a few minutes before reaching into his pocket for the ring. His hands trembled as he pulled it out. A vision of it bouncing out of the carriage and down a storm drain flashed through his mind, making him tighten his grip on the velvet box.

The blanket shifted as he turned to Erica, letting a cold gust of air into their warm cocoon.

"Hey, why did you—" Erica stopped complaining about the cold when she saw the ring in his hand. Her eyes widened, and her lips parted in surprise.

"Erica, I've loved you since the moment I kissed you under the mistletoe in our high school gym. Having you back in my life is the best thing that ever happened to me. I'll love you forever. I'll choose you forever. Will you marry me?"

Happy tears sparkled in Erica's eyes. "Yes! Yes, Cade, of course I will!"

Slowly, he slid the mitten off her left hand and slid the ring on. He knew she'd say yes to his proposal, but was relieved to see the ring was a perfect fit.

Erica held up her hand. She squealed in delight as the ring sparkled in the light from the streetlamps above.

It wasn't long before they reached their destination, a restaurant across from the park that Cade rented out for the evening.

"I have to call Julia, and my parents!" Erica said as he helped her out of the carriage.

Cade just grinned in response. He handed the driver a hefty tip, grateful the proposal went according to plan.

He stepped past Erica and opened the restaurant door, knowing exactly what waited for them on the other side.

"Congratulations!" Nate's voice boomed out over the rest as he and Erica stepped over the threshold.

∽

ERICA STOPPED IN THE DOORWAY, hands pressed to her cheeks in surprise. A flash went off as she surveyed the room in front of her. She couldn't believe he did all this. Cade had arranged the prefect proposal.

She floated on air as family and friends surrounded them with congratulatory words and hugs.

"I can't believe you're here!" she told Julia and Brad, who'd gotten married a few months before.

"Were you surprised?" Julia asked, her eyes alight with mischief. Her cousin loved knowing things before Erica.

"Yes!" Erica said, laughing. "I had no clue why he was dragging me through the snow in Central Park tonight."

Looking past Julia and Brad, she saw her parents, Nate and Ashley, and some of Cade's other college friends. Erica's friends were there, too—she even spotted Harrison and Pauline in the back.

She turned to Cade. "This is incredible. I can't believe you got so many people here without me finding out!"

Cade just grinned and planted a kiss on her forehead. "I was planning a proposal for an event planner. I knew it had to be good."

ACKNOWLEDGMENTS

To my readers—there are hundreds of holiday books out there. Thanks for spending time with mine.

To my friends, family and day-job colleagues—thanks for listening to me talk about writing a book for the last two years. I feel so blessed to be surrounded by such a supportive group of people. Thanks for asking how the writing's coming, understanding when I put writing ahead of hanging out, and reminding me to follow my dreams.

To my husband Chris—thanks for everything you do to give me time and space to write. Thanks for keeping me fed and taking on extra household chores, even though you work full-time, too. Thanks for taking Jax for walks so I can focus when I need to. You're the best. I love you.

Last, but certainly not least, a huge thank you to Stacy, my book coach. Your helpful suggestions and careful feedback were always spot on. Thank you for believing in my ability to tell this story. I couldn't have done it without you.

With Love,
Lynn

For inquiries or feedback, email me at lynnlarkinauthor@
gmail.com

facebook.com/lynnlarkinauthor
tiktok.com/@lynnlarkinauthor